I0575172

Yellow
MONKEY
PRESS

THE ETERNAL PREDICAMENT OF WILLIAM J. McCOY

A NOVELLA

YELLOW MONKEY PRESS
An Imprint of *Miniature Ginormous Media*
Arab, Alabama
YellowMonkeyPress@gmail.com

First edition October 2025

Printed by IngramSpark POD in the United States of America

Library of Congress Control Number: 2025917738

ISBN 979-8-9998427-0-1 (Hardcover)
ISBN 979-8-9998427-1-8 (Paperback)
ISBN 979-8-9998427-2-5 (ebook)
ISBN 979-8-9998427-3-2 (Audio Book)

www.JNoisLane.com

THE ETERNAL PREDICAMENT OF WILLIAM J. McCOY

A NOVELLA

J. NOIS LANE

For you, dear reader. You picked this book up, so you might as well see how it ends. And how it ends… well, that's for you to discover. With any luck, you'll find it mildly entertaining.

CHAPTER ONE

William J. McCoy looked nervously around the room, trying to find the waiter. He really needed that old-fashioned. He leaned forward and found Olivia McCoy's eyes across the table. Liv's laughter filled the room, her green eyes reflecting the dim glow of the lights hanging above the table. It was the same laughter he heard the day they'd first met.

"Really, Liv?" His right leg bounced faster than the rhythm of his heart.

She pushed a stray lock of auburn hair behind her ear, a smile lingering on her lips before it wavered slightly.

"Really," she said, her voice revealing a mixture of excitement and fear. Her eyes flicked away for a moment and then returned to his.

The old-fashioned arrived, but the words that came from his wife seconds before slowed the world down as he processed this revelation. Pregnant. They were having a kid. This was a new beginning, their beginning, and he felt ready to step into this new adventure with the woman seated in front of him. It seemed only natural since they had moved to Colorado less than a year prior. They had been married for a little over a year before that and decided to make the move from Kentucky. It was the first time either of them lived out of their home state. They soon settled into their first full-time adult jobs and bought their first house. Now it was time for another first.

"Parents?" He smiled and reached across the table, his fingers brushing hers. "That's . . . that's amazing!" He leaned forward and kissed her, the brief moment followed by hesitation as he leaned his forehead to hers.

"You're scared." Her voice was a whisper, barely cutting through the clatter of plates and the muffled conversations, but somehow it felt like the world had quieted just for them.

"Terrified." His hand tightened around hers. He swallowed, then forced a smile. "But I'm excited too. We'll figure this out. Together."

Her eyes searched his. "Promise?"

"Cross my heart and hope to die."

"Stick a needle in your eye?"

He gave her a crooked smile, as the love of his life drew him to the surface. "Only if it gets me out of changing diapers."

That earned a soft chuckle from her, the release of a breath he didn't realize she'd been holding.

They sat there, holding hands, the rest of the world fading into nothingness. Just William and Liv, and the life they were about to bring into the world. No hesitation, no looking back. They were just two souls hitched together for the ride, whatever came next.

Liv's smile lit up the car. Her joy was impossible to resist, spreading warmth like a wildfire that cut through the evening chill seeping in from outside. Her glow matched her excitement as much as her hair matched the glow of the setting sun.

"Okay. I need to work on my dad jokes if I'm going to be a dad." He put one hand on the steering wheel and his other hand on hers beside him.

Liv gave him a side-eye. "Please don't. I love you, but I'm pretty sure dad jokes are grounds for divorce."

"A turkey walks into a bar."

"No!" She groaned, throwing her head back. Her smile was gone, but her eyes were showing the truth. She was happier than she had ever been.

"The bartender takes one look at the turkey and says—"

"I swear, if you finish that sentence, you're sleeping on the couch tonight."

He had a sly smile on his face. "We don't serve food here."

Liv stared at him for a second and clearly tried to look serious, but she lost the battle. She let out a snort as she laughed. "That's the dumbest joke I've ever heard!"

Willliam squeezed her hand. "That's how I know you love me."

"Oh, you're gonna see how much I love you over the next few months! When you see what happens to my body. What I'm gonna sacrifice to give you this child. Mister, you're gonna see! And I'm gonna see how much you love me when I send you out at three in the morning for watermelon in February!"

William brought her hand to his mouth and kissed it.

"Can you believe it?" Liv held his hand tighter. "I'm imagining tiny boots, onesies with bears on them, and oh . . . teaching her to bake a cake!"

"Or how to throw a baseball," William added, winking at her as he looked in the rearview mirror. He took the curves of the winding mountain road like he knew every twist of asphalt by heart.

"Let's not get ahead of ourselves." Liv playfully nudged his shoulder. "We don't even know if it's a boy or a girl. But let's pick out names for both. Just to be prepared."

"Names? How about something classic? Like William Jr. if it's a boy or for a girl maybe . . . "

The rest of his sentence was stolen by a sharp pop. The steering wheel jerked violently in his hands as he tightened his grip. The car lurched and the tires screeched against the pavement.

"William!" Liv's voice spiked with panic as she clutched the armrest.

William's muscles tensed, adrenaline taking over. The car swayed as the metal wheel from the blown tire hit the asphalt. William panicked and turned the steering wheel away from the guardrail, then immediately knew he had made a mistake.

"Shit, shit, shit," he muttered under his breath, white-knuckling the steering wheel. His foot glued the brake to the floor, as he desperately tried in vain to make the car stop. The car had other plans and fishtailed.

The passenger side of the car slammed into the guardrail, glass exploding around Liv. William turned his head just in time to see the guardrail crumple, still unable to stop the car's momentum. Liv's eyes widened in terror, her gaze locked on William as tears blurred his vision. She reached for William as everything seemed to freeze around them. The screeching metal slowed to a drawn-out wail until the car slammed into the earth, then rolled as it continued down the embankment. With the crunch of metal, William focused on Liv's face, her beauty standing out among the chaos, and in those moments, he knew it was goodbye.

The car slammed against a tree, bringing deafening silence as everything went dark.

CHAPTER TWO

Pain met William before he could even register where he was. He blinked and squinted against the fluorescent lights, each breath feeling like someone was punching him in his ribs. The consistent beeping of medical equipment started to clear his disorientation. His vision swam as he turned his head slightly before the pain stopped him.

Then like a flood, it all came rushing back to him. With it came a wave of panic.

"Hello?" His voice startled him as it croaked, raspy with fear and urgency. "Liv . . . my wife, where is my wife?"

His throat felt like he'd swallowed sandpaper, but he didn't care. William shifted, trying to sit up despite the pain lancing through him, the need to know about Liv driving him more than the instinct for self-preservation. Each second felt like he was about to get news he wasn't sure he could handle.

"Mr. McCoy, please lie back," a nurse said, appearing at his side with a calm that irritated him.

"Liv. Where is she? Is she okay?" William gripped the nurse's arm with more strength than he meant to use. Her scrubs were a blur of color in his still-adjusting sight, but her face was clear.

"Sir, you need to rest. Your body has been through a lot," She tried to ease his grip, but William clung on despite not being able to rise off the bed.

His body screamed at him to stop trying to move.

"Please! Tell me about my wife!" The desperation in his voice was raw, wanting to get straight to the point. "I need to know if she's . . ." He couldn't finish the sentence; the possibility was too much. He began to cry.

"Mr. McCoy, please," the nurse tried again, but William cut her off.

"Is she alive?" The words came out in a mumble as he let go of the nurse's arm. Each second without an answer stretched into an eternity.

She clearly didn't know what to say, and her eyes started to tear up as a doctor entered the room. He was young but carried himself with purpose. William's heart, already frantic, threatened to burst through his rib cage, desperate for the answer he already knew.

"Mr. McCoy, I'm Dr. Peterson." His voice was devoid of the warmth one might hope for in such a situation. "We need to check your vitals and go over your injuries, but I know you understandably want to know about your wife first. I'm afraid I have some . . . unfortunate news."

William hung on to the pause from the doctor, waiting for the inevitable but still desperate not to let go of the small piece of hope that kept him from spiraling into insanity.

"Your wife . . ." The doctor paused again, the gravity of the situation showing a chink in the doctor's armor as some emotion came through. "She didn't make it. I'm . . . I'm so sorry."

"Didn't make it?" William's head swirled as the doctor's words refused to take root in his mind. "What do you mean she didn't make it? That's bullshit!"

"Mr. McCoy . . ."

"Stop! Just stop!" Rage flooded William's veins. Liv couldn't be dead. This had to be a mistake. A twisted, terrible mistake. He threw back the hospital sheets, not caring about his bruised body or the IV lines tugging at his skin.

"Sir, you need to stay in bed. Your injuries . . ." Dr. Peterson said, but William wasn't listening.

"Get out of my way!" He tried to swing his legs over the side of the bed, not noticing his left leg was in a temporary walking boot. As soon as his leg moved, it sent him backward onto the bed in agony.

"Mr. McCoy, please!" But the doctor's plea was interrupted as the nurse rushed forward to try to restrain William. "I've got him," Dr. Peterson said as he beat the nurse to it.

William let out a determined yell. Though intent on leaving, he also didn't know how he was going to be successful doing that because the room wouldn't stop spinning long enough for him to get out of bed in the first place. The more he tried to get up, the more the room spun. And the pain. That wasn't helping either.

"Sedate him! Propofol, twenty milligrams!" Dr. Peterson said.

The nurse rushed from the room and was back in seconds. Their words became muffled, distant, drowned out by the roaring in William's ears and the shattering of his world. Without Liv, there was no world worth living in.

William slowly opened his eyes. He was in a different room than before. He now had a window showing a picturesque sunset sky behind the Colorado Front Range. The room was dimly lit, and the air held a subtle whiff of cigar smoke that pulled him back slowly to the surface. The scent was the same brand his father used to smoke on special occasions with a bit of scotch. One of those special occasions was the night before William and Liv's wedding day.

"Remember, son," his father had said as he held a lit cigar between his fingers, a crystal glass of amber scotch in his other hand. "It's all about the pairing. If you match the right cigar with the right scotch, you find heaven. There's nothing like it."

The memory was so vivid that for a heartbeat William forgot the crushing weight of his loss. The rich, smoky aroma wrapped around him, a comforting embrace reminding him of a time when happiness wasn't just something fleeting on the edge of his reality.

He clung to the memory, trying to allow it to push his grief far enough into the recesses of his soul that he wouldn't have to remember. It was all in vain, however, as tears welled up and spilled out in an eruption of sorrow. William choked back a sob as his body wanted to curl up in a ball, his muscles tensing. His body was still drunk on pain, but something was off. His arms wouldn't obey the commands from his brain. He felt his muscles constrict, but nothing moved. He looked at his hands to see straps hugging his wrists, and lower down he could feel the same with his legs.

"Son of a . . ." He grunted, pulling against the restraints and letting out a scream. They held fast, and the frustrating strain of his weakened muscles caused his arms to shake. He gave up, closed his eyes, and tried to slow his breathing. But he saw Liv and her beautiful smile, which dug a thick, heavy hole in his chest. It welled up and felt like it was about to burst out of his throat. He couldn't hold it back, so he gave way to another flood of tears and sobbed in agony.

"Why?" As the word escaped his lips, he felt his very soul rip. The question hung in the air, and he wasn't sure if it was a question or an accusation, or maybe even a plea.

"That would be where I come in."

CHAPTER THREE

William stiffened, his heart racing. It was a man's voice. His voice sounded older and gritty from years of smoking. Looking around the room, the shadows didn't reveal the source of the voice.

"Who's there?"

"Oh, I'm sorry. That's my fault."

William's eyes stopped. There, nestled in the corner of the room, a silhouette moved and brought the glowing red ember of a cigar to its mouth. As he puffed on the cigar, the ember grew brighter, then was dimmed by bellowing smoke being blown out of the stranger's mouth. The sight sent William's mind reeling with a mixture of fear and the raw edge of recent loss.

"Who are you?" William's eyes narrowed on the figure.

"Hello, William," the old man said, smoke enveloping the silhouette. He stood, and the light caught a glint of unnatural red in his eyes.

"Who are you? How do you know my name?"

The old man let out a chuckle. He adjusted the brim of his homburg hat as he walked to the foot of William's bed. He dusted off his tweed suit and brushed his bowtie with one hand. "This is always my favorite part." He smiled from ear to ear as he put his cigar between his teeth. The wrinkles on the old man's face stretched as he smiled, hinting at a youth that had passed long ago.

William opened his mouth to speak, but nothing came out. He swallowed and tried again.

"What? What are you talking about? Do I know you?" William wasn't sure, but something was nagging at him that he might. He was, after all, coming out of being sedated. He couldn't think straight. "It seems like I might know you . . . maybe?"

"This is absolutely my favorite part," he said as he pointed at William, "but you wouldn't know that." He pulled a handkerchief from his coat pocket, wiped his eyes, and put the handkerchief back. "Nor would you remember me. What would you say if I told you that you have lived many lives before this one, and in each one of those lives, we have had this exact conversation? You and me."

"Okay . . . I think I'm going to call the nurse now."

William looked for the nurse call button and found it on the inside of the bed rail. He tried to reach for it, but with the straps holding him down, it was just out of reach. "Damn it!"

"Here, allow me." The old man walked over and pushed the nurse call button. The little light illuminated beside the clip-art picture of a nurse. "There you go, but they won't come. Not now anyway." His smile was gone as he took another puff of his cigar. He leaned down and blew smoke toward William. "I'm not hitting the sauce either." The old man straightened. "At least not right now." His smile returned with a chuckle.

"Look, mister, I just lost my wife, so I'm not in the mood, okay? I don't know if you're turned around or think I'm someone else or what. But would you please just leave? The smoke is bothering me." William became a bit puzzled just then. "And how the hell are you even smoking that thing in here without the smoke alarm going off?"

The old man shrugged. "Listen, kid, I understand you're hurting. Your wife was a wonderful person. You loved her, and she was the light of your life: the perfect pairing. She was wha—"

"What did you say?"

The old man smiled, and his eyes grew narrow. "Just like the right cigar and scotch." Sticking his cigar in his mouth, he winked. "Heaven."

"Who are you? What's your name?"

He stood there looking taller than he should have. For an old man, he stood with strength and didn't hold himself the way a man his age normally would. There was no slouching or slumping. His appearance otherwise leaned toward him pushing ninety; at least.

"I'm someone who is tired of all of this." The old man gestured around the room and then took another puff of his cigar. "It's time for a change."

William looked at the nurse call button and tried again to reach it with no success.

"Stop that! I told you they won't come!"

Irritation laced the old man's voice. William froze as the eyes that stared back at him turned red and stayed red for a good five seconds or so. Dread crept over William and sent a chill through his body.

"I know you don't remember me or your past lives, but I remember. I remember you. I remember Liv. I remember it all." He turned and walked back to the foot of the bed. "You can call me Ivan."

"Your eyes . . . they . . ." William said.

"I mention that I've known you in past lives, plural lives, and you want to ask about my eyes?" Ivan chuckled. His demeanor lightened again. "That's what I like about you, William, you never change. It's always the eyes."

Ivan put his cigar in his mouth and straightened his suit coat with both hands. He then pulled the cigar from his mouth and in a very steady, static, and proud tone said, "I'm a demon. You heard me correctly. A demon. Your name is William J. McCoy. Your wife, Olivia McCoy, goes by Liv, was recently killed in an automobile accident. You have lived many lives before this one, and in each one the same thing happens: you meet Liv, and a short time later, she dies. You will have to live this moment in countless more lives, each time having no memory of the previous life or the events of that previous life."

It was a perfect speech he had rattled off many times before. That was clear. Ivan let out a breath and added, "But I'm tired, William. We've been doing this, the same thing, for such a long time. I'm simply tired of it. It's now become boring to me."

William looked at Ivan with his mouth open. Fear encompassed him. This couldn't really be a demon. Ivan looked like a harmless old man. Well, as harmless as secondhand smoke could be. It was the eyes, though. When they turned red, every hair on William's head stood on end. The nurses weren't answering, and the room was so full of smoke there was no way the fire alarm wouldn't go off. Yet it wasn't.

And strangely, something did seem familiar with all of this. It was like a memory that had slipped out of reach to a point he couldn't recall, no matter how hard he tried. His brain told him to scream at the top of his lungs for help, yet every bone in his body told him Ivan was telling the truth. The only thing William could spit out was, "How?"

"How?" Ivan chuckled. "Normally you ask 'why?'"

"That too!" William said, his eyes wide.

"I'll tell you both. How about that? Since we're changing things up this go-around!" Ivan said. "I don't want to tell you too much, though. That would ruin any fun this is going to be." Ivan tilted his hat back. "In actuality, the answer is the same to both 'why' and 'how.' It's simple: because I can. I'd like to offer you a sliver of hope amid this cesspool of a world. What if I told you that you have a chance to change things? You could bring back what you've lost?" Ivan took a puff of his cigar.

"Is this some sort of game to you?"

"Life is the game, my dear boy." His tone was light but carried dark undertones. "Death, however, is the wild card. And I am rather good at playing those."

"What do you mean? You cause death?"

"You see, William, I have control over your life and your wife's life. We, you and I, made a deal a very long time ago. I can influence you and your decisions without you even knowing about it. And I have. In fact, about thirty-three times now, I have orchestrated your wife's death and made sure it happened right in front of your eyes. Every time. I have never failed." He paused, and he seemed to reflect on something for a moment. "But make no mistake, you do make your own choices. I'm not a puppet master."

William's face grew hot with anger. "Not a puppet master? If you do this to Liv and me over and over, isn't that exactly what you are? How do we make our own choices if that is, in fact, what you do?" William felt lightheaded as he continued. "Is this some kind of sick joke? What you're telling me is not only impossible, it's pure fantasy! It's twisted, and you're insane!"

"Is it?" Ivan looked curious. "Impossible? I haven't noticed. Let me assure you, it's certainly possible because I've done it to you. Many times. Is it sick? Is it a joke? Perhaps."

He walked back over to William's bedside and sighed. "I know you don't fully believe me, what I'm telling you. You never do. We have this same conversation each time, and you never believe me."

He pointed at William with his cigar. "You love your wife, and you would do anything for her, yeah?"

William looked up at Ivan.

"What would you say if I told you I can give you one chance to save your wife's life?" Ivan held up one finger as he puffed on his cigar. "Instead of you lying here strapped to this hospital bed, Liv would be alive. Right here, right now. And not only that." Ivan pulled the cigar from his mouth and blew out a puff of smoke. "I will stop this endless cycle of her dying, life after life." Ivan's smile came back and his eyes glimmered red again.

"How's that even possible?"

"Don't worry about that. All you need to worry about is your plan to save Liv." There was a moment of concern on Ivan's face, and then it was gone. "I will put you back in a past life of yours, a life of my choosing, just so we're clear. If you save her in that life, you will save her in this life. But there's a catch."

"No, really? Imagine that."

Ivan chuckled and pointed at William as if they were best friends, jesting with each other. "You get me, you really do!" He cleared his throat and said, "Seriously, though, you will only have memories of this life. I can't make it too easy for you. If you fail to save her, you will find yourself back in this hospital bed, and I'll see you in your next life, ready to do this all over again."

"If you're so tired of all of this, why don't you just stop making her die? Why not just leave us alone? Or better yet, if you have all this power, why not just bring her back to life or turn back time and stop her from dying in the first place?"

Ivan leaned close to the bed, and William could smell his breath, which smelled of pure sulfur. "Well, William, because you're forgetting one very important thing. As I already told you, I am a demon." As Ivan said the last word, his eyes glowed red, and William flinched.

The room began to spin again, or so it felt to William. His senses betrayed him and went into overdrive as his nostrils filled with the scent of pine from a forest. William could see his breath, and he shivered. With a chuckle, Ivan stood straight and looked at the ceiling. His eyes illuminated the room with a red hue. William looked up, and the hospital ceiling was gone. It just wasn't there. Instead, he saw the night sky, clear and full of stars.

William looked in disbelief at Ivan, and Ivan looked back at him with glowing red eyes. His heart thundered as he pulled on the bed straps as hard as he could. Ivan laughed hysterically, and he flicked his cigar at William.

CHAPTER FOUR

William's mind was a jumbled mess of images: shattered glass, Liv's laughter, Ivan's red eyes. None of it, however, made sense against the backdrop of where he found himself.

He sat with his back against a tree in the woods. The moonlit autumn air bit at his skin, and leaves crunched under him as he shifted to the side. The smell brought back childhood memories of deer hunting with his grandfather.

"What the hell?" His whisper was hoarse.

William tried to push himself to his feet, but his body protested with a dizzying weakness that forced him back to the ground. "Great. Just great."

With effort, he made his way to his feet, propping himself on shaking arms against the tree. He looked around but couldn't make anything out in the shadows staring back at him.

"This can't be real." He patted his sides, noticing the coarse fabric. It felt stiff and rough, reminding him of dirty burlap or an itchy jean material. "What is this?"

"The Old South at night. There's nothing like it, Willie!"

William jumped at Ivan's voice cracking through the silence.

"What have you done, old man? Did you drug me and drag me out here to the woods?"

Ivan chuckled. "What you're wearing, that's your uniform . . . sort of. Your mother made it for you when you left home to fight in the war. I told you, this is one of your past lives. This is a chance to save Liv." Ivan puffed on his cigar while admiring the uniform William wore.

William felt the dizziness leave, and he stood on his own as his strength returned. "No pain?" He moved his head from side to side and tilted his neck. "This . . . this is remarkable. A few moments ago, I was in a hospital bed hurting in places I didn't even know existed. Now, well, the only things hurting are my feet." William lifted one of his feet to examine his boots.

"Yes," Ivan said. "This isn't the body you were just in. This is a different body. Your name in this life is Noah Wheaton, and you've been walking quite a long way for quite a long time."

"Wait a minute. You said I'm wearing a uniform, and you said something about the Old South. And a war. What war? What year is it?" William felt a sudden chill as ice flowed through his veins.

"Relax, my boy. It's October 1866. The war is over. At least officially. You know as well as I do that even in your day, some in the South still believe the war rages on. 'The South will rise again' and all." Ivan said that last part in a perfectly executed Southern gentleman's accent.

"You were telling the truth? You sent me back in time?"

Ivan flicked the ash from his cigar and looked at William. "Well, it's not exactly time travel per se."

"What? What does that mean? What is this then? Am I dreaming?"

"A story for another time, my boy." Ivan dropped his cigar butt to the ground and stepped on it to put it out.

"Don't call me 'my boy.' I don't know you, and I certainly don't trust you. We are not friends. If this is real, that means you really are the reason Liv is dead. You said in every life Liv dies, and I'm left alone to deal with it. Over and over."

Anger consumed William, and he walked right up to Ivan. He looked into the black of Ivan's eyes and suddenly realized they were the same height. After a moment, with all the strength he could gather, William reared back and put everything he had into a punch toward Ivan's face. Ivan vanished as William's fist flew at him. The momentum of the punch pulled William forward, and he fell on the leaf-covered ground.

"I'm only trying to help you, William." Ivan reappeared right where he'd previously stood.

William screamed in frustration. "Help me? If you really wanted to help me and you have the power to do what you say you can do, why don't you just turn back time and save Liv? Stop us from getting into our car? You know, make the car not crank, stop the tire from blowing? Something more simple! Why this?"

"Where's the fun in that?" Ivan's eyes glowed red for a second and then faded. "You don't have any choice, son. You are here. You might as well try and save Liv. Stop her from dying in this life, and I'll keep my word."

They looked at each other, each waiting for the other to make the first move. William couldn't trust Ivan. Ivan knew that but likely didn't care.

"If I knew how to kill you, I would. Believe me. Every part of me hates you. But if you can help me save Liv so she and our child are okay, then . . ." A light clicked on in William's mind. "If I'm in Noah's body, where is he? Is he in my body in the future?"

Ivan sighed and said, "Now, come on, kid! You've been watching too many TV shows. Your consciousness is his consciousness; you just don't remember. You are the same person now as you are in every life. Look, think of it like having a bad memory. You just can't remember Noah's life."

"A bad memory?" William got an idea. "Is there a way you can unlock this 'bad memory' so I know where I am and what I'm supposed to do to save Liv?"

"Nice try! But no cigar," Ivan said. "Besides, it's a wonderful thing to have a bad memory. It's your biggest advantage here."

"Why would that be my biggest advantage?"

"The best thing about a bad memory in this situation is you get to enjoy so many things, good things, for the first time, all over again. Think about it. The first time you met Liv, how wonderful it was. Think about how it made you feel. I don't want to rob you of something so beautiful in this life."

"Bullshit! You just don't want me to remember how she dies in this life so I can't save her. You want me to fail so you can continue to get your jollies off from me running around here trying to save her, making a fool of myself, and destroying my soul in the process." William felt defeated. "I can't bear to live through her dying again. Please."

For a moment, Ivan looked as if he might actually have a heart. He held his hands up in surrender. "Okay. Cards on the table, kid. Truth be known, I'm breaking some rules by putting you back in this life. While I can do that, I can't unblock your mind. Even if I wanted to. Scout's honor." Ivan held up three fingers and chuckled.

"I don't believe you, but even if I did, either way, how do I know you can bring Liv back? How do I know this isn't some new aspect of your sick game? Something else for your amusement? In your words, you're a demon. If I save her, how do I know you'll keep your word?"

"You don't. But don't you love her enough to try?"

"Seeing her again for even a moment is worth any hell you can put me through."

"My God, boy! Then let's get to it! There's one thing I know, and it's how to put you through hell!"

William strode up to Ivan again as anger and courage rushed through his veins.

"Even if you could, you wouldn't want to," Ivan said and disappeared.

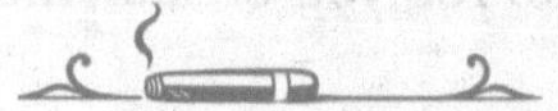

A few moments later, William sat back down against the same tree that had welcomed him to 1866 and noticed a small worn knapsack beside it. Fumbling through it, he found some letters, a knife, two apples, and a rolled-up piece of paper. It was too dark to read the letters or the roll of paper, so he put everything back and decided he would figure out where he was exactly in the morning, once there was light to see.

If he and Liv met in this life, and she was meant to die this time too, then he would play the part. He'd find her and save her.

CHAPTER FIVE

W illiam's face was met by the warmth of the morning sun. He had found it hard to fall asleep and couldn't stop thinking of Liv and replaying the car crash over and over in his mind. What could he have done differently? His cheeks stung from the mixture of the cold morning air and dried tears.

He looked around, and the landscape of trees in front of him was a sight so ordinary and plain it was like a slap to the face. Then, turning to look behind him, not ten yards from where he'd spent the night, was the road. An actual dirt road of two wagon-wheel ruts with brown grass in between.

"Really?"

He grabbed the knapsack and fished out an apple to feed the hunger that had crept in. As he ate, he pulled out the envelopes. They appeared to have been read many times, perhaps Noah's way of dealing with being homesick. Reading through them, he pieced together that he was from a town named New Rescue in northern Alabama. The contents of the letters spoke of a life foreign to him, but they also brought up a longing from deep inside, as if he were reuniting with a lost part of his soul. They were all signed

"Your loving mother." The envelopes held no return address or name of the sender.

He unrolled the roll of paper, and it revealed a crude certificate showing his signature as "Noah L. Wheaton." The certificate read:

> *"I, Noah L. Wheaton of the state of Alabama, do solemnly swear to affirm, in the presence of Almighty God, that I will henceforth faithfully support, protect, and defend the Constitution of the United States and the Union of the states thereunder; and I will, in like manner, abide by and faithfully support all laws and proclamations which have been made during the existing rebellion with reference to the emancipation of slaves. So help me God.*
>
> *Sworn and subscribed to on this 10th day of June 1865 AD, before A. J. Hunting, JP."*

"Well, all right," William said to himself as he placed the certificate and letters back into the knapsack.

Hauling himself to his feet with more anger than energy, the road seemed to mock him with its simplicity. Cursing under his breath, William brushed off the leaves from his clothes and stepped through the tree line onto the road. He looked left and saw the road led to a murky brown river where a single flat ferryboat sat by a dock. Headed his way, still a long way off, was a wagon. He looked to the right and saw the road led to a mountain, started to ascend, and then curved to the right.

A pull in his chest, vague yet insistent, steered him away from the river and toward the mountain ascent. The road was a scar across the land, familiar in a way that made his heart itch. "Guess we're headed upward." He grunted, muscles tensing in anticipation as he set off.

His boots scuffed the dirt, kicking up little puffs of dust as the road tilted upward. What felt like an hour later was only about half that when William realized the far-off wagon had caught up to him. He stepped to the side to let it pass.

"Hey, you there! Wait a minute!"

William turned to see the wagon that had been a distant speck before now up close. With a creak of wood and a jangle of the harness, it came to a halt beside him. The driver, a slender man about thirty years old, looked at him as if he were looking at a ghost. The man smiled, revealing some gaps where teeth should have been, then jumped from the wagon and embraced William.

"I'll be damned . . . Noah! It is you!" The driver was more than excited, staring at William with a mix of shock and joy. "Your mama's gonna be so glad to see you!"

William's mind raced, not knowing what to do or say, but apparently, this man knew Noah and his mama. William smiled back. "Yeah, thought I'd surprise her."

"We all thought you were dead! Come on, hop on!" The man's voice demanded no argument, a command born from relief rather than authority. "You can tell me about fightin' them Yanks on the way home! It's an honor to help out my cousin! One of Bama's bravest!"

"Sure," William said, masking his confusion with emotions he didn't feel. He hoisted himself onto the wagon, the wood creaking in protest under his weight. "Wouldn't want to disappoint."

The wagon was just a simple rectangular box, flat and open. William's newfound cousin didn't seem to be hauling much, as the wagon bed was all but bare. He worried about how this was going to work. Ivan didn't give him much to go on, and now he had a cousin offering to give him a lift home, a cousin whose name he didn't know, and he was sure it would be strange if he asked.

His cousin reached behind the seat and pulled out a ladle filled with water from a bucket. The sight made William realize how thirsty he was. His cousin held it out, and William gratefully took it. "Thanks!"

"It's nothin'." The cousin cleared his throat and spat to the side.

William coughed as the water burned going down. It tasted like he was drinking pure gasoline. "That's not water!"

His cousin laughed hysterically. "Come on, Noah! You lost your taste for my moonshine? You always said it was the best on the mountain!"

"No, no," William said. He coughed again to try to ease the burning. "It's still great. I was just expecting water. That's all."

With a click of his tongue, the cousin had the mule pulling the wagon up the mountain road. The wagon didn't move much faster than William could walk, but at least he was off his feet. His cousin looked over at him with eyes hungry for a good story. "Tell me everything! How'd you manage to come out alive? The last we heard, you were taken captive near Chattanooga. Somethin' like, maybe, two years ago. But when them Yanks let everyone go from around there, you weren't with them. All we could do was figure they had you hung or shot or somethin' like that."

"I, uh, I honestly don't remember." William shrugged. "Everything about the war . . . it's like it was all wiped away." William fixed his gaze on the winding path ahead, each turn of the road bringing him closer to Liv. He just had to survive the world's most awkward wagon ride to get to her.

"Huh. Most of the boys coming home say the war haunts them damn well every night. They wake up screamin' as if the devil himself was chasing them."

"Yeah? The devil? That part I can relate to."

The wagon lurched forward, and William gripped the wooden side to keep his balance. The cousin clicked his tongue twice, and the mule picked up its pace.

They rode in uncomfortable silence for a while. The rhythmic sound of the mule's hooves and the wagon moving along soothed the storm inside William's mind. Every thought was about Liv and finding her. His task felt hopeless with nothing to give him direction.

"Reckon the whole community's been turned on its head since you've been gone," his driver said. "Union boys set up camp on the back side of the mountain, by the niter caves. Then moved into town and took over. Confederate dollars ain't worth the paper they printed on anymore. Greenbacks or barter's the way now."

"Sounds like a big mess," William replied without any emotion, his gaze tracing the horizon. "What's a niter cave?"

"Lord Almighty, Noah! The niter! The niter we used to make powder? For our guns? In the caves down in the cove. Where we played growing up!"

William suddenly remembered. They had saltpeter in Kentucky where he grew up. It was one component, a major one, used to make gunpowder. "Nitrate! You mean nitrate, right?"

"That's what I done said! Shit, Noah! The war sure did scramble your noggin!"

"It's like I'm a completely different person, I know. Believe me, I know. Things are a bit fuzzy to me. So, maybe humor me? Is there anyone around town with red hair? A girl about my age? She would be single. I need to find her."

His cousin shook his head. "Nah. Never seen any grown women with red hair around here. But there have been a few new folks settle near the caves. They showed up right after you up and left. They all worked the caves until the Yanks came in and put a stop to it."

"Do you know where those people are now? You have to take me to them! Who I'm looking for might be with them."

His cousin looked over at him, puzzled. "Something ain't right with you. You have some fancy new words and way of talkin'. And what about your ma? She thinks you're dead, Noah! You need to go see your ma before you do anything." The look on his face was sincere and determined.

William understood what his cousin was saying, and he could see there was going to be no other way. He was reminded of where he was raised; these people sounded just like the ones he'd grown up around. Family came first, and nothing was ever allowed to get in the way. He got it. But to William, Liv was his family. She was his wife. How could he explain to this man sitting beside him, driving a mule-drawn wagon up a country mountain road that he was from the future? And being tortured by a demon on top of it all? He doubted it would go over well. He wondered if they burned people at the stake in 1866 Alabama.

He felt a growing compulsion to ask about Noah's mother. "How is Ma?"

Thomas said, "She's been holding things together the best she can, what with your pa . . ."

He trailed off and didn't finish the thought. William felt a pang of guilt and sorrow that wasn't his to claim, and he barely noticed the creak of the wagon as it made its way along the mountain road. His mind churned with a storm of thoughts, each one colliding with the next in a chaos of urgency and dread. The longing that pulled him to this path twisted inside him now, turning into a sharp need clenching his gut. Why were his feelings for Noah's mother competing with his need to find Liv? He didn't know what was happening with his emotions, but he couldn't let anything detour him from finding Liv. If Noah was trying to break through, William had to fight it.

"I'm sorry," William said, his voice betraying his attempt to conceal the inner tension, "I need to find this girl."

His cousin's eyes flicked from the road to William. His brows knitted together, the joy of a blessed reunion changing into something else. "This girl?" The tension hung between them like a neon sign.

"Yeah, this redheaded girl." William's knuckles were white as he gripped the wooden seat. "Can't explain it all. It wouldn't make any sense, but I've gotta find her. Fast."

"Slow down, Noah." The cousin's voice was a mix of confusion and caution. "Mildred Wheaton is one of the strongest women I've ever known. I'm proud to be her nephew. But you gotta know, your ma is hurtin'. She thinks you're dead. Seeing you will bring light back to her soul. She hasn't been the same since you left. Don't that mean somethin' to you?"

Mildred. The name made his heart ache, and his words got caught in his throat.

"Of course it does," William said, more sharply than he'd intended. Where'd that come from? "But there's things, complicated things, you wouldn't understand."

"Try me." His tone held a hint of steel.

William's jaw tightened. He wasn't Noah; he couldn't lean on shared memories or explain the web of fate Ivan had spun around him. He wasn't going to get any useful information about Liv from his cousin. He decided to wait until he got to Noah's home and see if his mother knew anything. Women in small communities talked, which meant they usually knew more about what was going on than anyone else anyway.

His cousin's face relayed that he knew he'd won. "We've been livin' in the belly of it since the Yanks decided to stick around. What's one more problem among the rest? We fought a war so they couldn't tell us what we can and cannot do." He spat to the side of the wagon. "Seems like they gonna tell us what to do all the same. They are callin' it 'reconstruction,' I'm told. If you ask me, and none has, it's just a fancy word for pushing us around!"

William had heard about Reconstruction in high school American History class. He hadn't paid much attention then, although now he wished he had. Because of that, it didn't take too much for him to play dumb.

"What do you mean, reconstruction? What are they doing?"

"Well, we got word two weeks ago they installed one of their own in Montgomery. A General Swayne, I think. Don't matter, no fat cat in the capital ever cared enough about us mountain folk anyhow. We got our own things to deal with, seeing how Captain Sacks set up camp with a few soldiers on the main road in town. He's even telling us we have to rename the town Union Hill. Can you imagine? We ain't on no damn hill! They just trying to . . . uh, what's the word?"

"Demoralize. They're trying to take away your pride," William said. He felt his cousin's pain. He felt the same way now after learning about Ivan. How could his life have been influenced by an unseen, unknown demon? No, he refused to believe it. He and Liv were soulmates. They loved each other, and no demon was responsible for that. Not for something so beautiful and special. He would find a way to save her and end this.

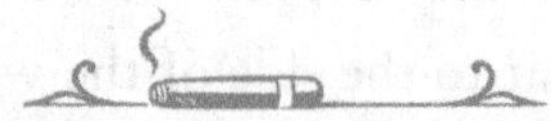

The wagon crested the top of the mountain, revealing a seemingly never-ending flat plateau. He looked behind him and saw a carpet of red, orange, and yellow trees laid out below, stretching to the river he'd seen earlier.

"Wow! That's one of the most beautiful views I've ever seen."

His cousin turned and looked. "Hmm. I suppose the Almighty knew what He was doing."

As the wagon came to the town of New Rescue, William noticed how small it was. There were only a handful of buildings on each side of the road, with horses and a few wagons milling around. It almost reminded him of towns in a Western film, except there were a lot of Union soldiers in blue coats around. Some were in small groups talking, and others were busy with various tasks. As their wagon rolled past, they looked up and stared. It made William feel uneasy. He wished he had a change of clothes and wasn't wearing his uniform. He reached into the knapsack slung around his chest and clutched the knife inside without pulling it out.

Even the people in normal civilian clothing were staring; however, some of them were whispering to each other. This made William feel a little less on edge about the soldiers, and he let go of the knife, but it still made him feel awkward.

"I told you. We all thought you was dead."

"Yeah, looks like I'm the talk of the town."

"Better you than me. I reckon you better change clothes first chance you get."

"The thought already crossed my mind."

William couldn't imagine living through this. It had to feel like an invading army taking over their life. Occupying their world without permission. It was good the war was over and the North had won. Slavery was wrong, and no man, woman, or child should ever have been treated the way they were treated. Looking around, though, William didn't see many who could even have afforded a slave if they wanted to. These people looked like nothing more than simple farmers; country folks just trying to get by. He wondered how much this town had changed between now and his own day. Was it still this small? Did these kinds of salt-of-the-earth people still reside there? Did it even still exist?

As they made their way to the other edge of the town, Noah's cousin guided the wagon to the right and stopped in front of a small green house sitting on a hill. Several chickens were running around the yard with a few ducks. One lone goose honked and chased a chicken around the corner of the house. The ground was littered with pecans that had fallen from the two enormous trees that sat like two guards in front of the house. The wagon's wheels crushed a few of the nuts as it rolled to a stop.

Off to the side of the house was a stone well sitting against a fence surrounding a good-sized garden. Most of the crops had been harvested already, from the looks of things, but there were a few plants still there, as well as brown, dried-out cornstalks along the far end of the garden. The smell was undeniable. It was a country farm. The kind that provided for its inhabitants as long as they put the work in.

William hopped out of the wagon and thanked his cousin for the ride.

"Think nothin' of it. Now, go on." He nodded toward the house where Noah's mother already stood by the front door. "She's been waitin' longer than any mama should. I have to get on home before my own ma starts to worry. We'll come around soon and welcome y'all home somethin' proper," his cousin said as he gestured to the back of his wagon where the moonshine sat.

When he was alone in the yard, William's heart welled up with the feeling of home. He felt like he had been gone for far too long and now he was returning to where he belonged. It was strange because his mind said this was a place he'd never seen before, yet his soul ached to be here.

"Shit, Ivan. What have you done to me?"

He looked toward Noah's mother, Mildred. She was an older woman, but she rushed off the steps of the porch as fast as her legs would carry her. She appeared to be in her early to mid-sixties and wore a dark green flowered dress with a dirty apron tied around her waist. On her head was a yellow bonnet covering gray hair that still showed a bit of brown here and there. As her feet hit the grass, she screamed, "Noah! Oh, thank God! You're alive!"

The woman ran faster than William would have thought possible and swallowed him up in her embrace. "I never could have imagined this day would come! You're my heart walking outside my body, son. It was lost without you here!"

William's chest swelled. This was all strange to him. His mother looked straight into his eyes with a smile of approval and happiness. Tears welled up and started to fall from her eyes. He looked away, all of this too real. Until now, he still held out hope this was possibly just a vivid dream. Tears flowed from his own eyes, and he returned her embrace. His face showed the confusion that raced through his mind.

She smiled and said, "You look weary! And way too skinny! Come on, I'll get you a bite to eat." She took him by the arm. "Was that Thomas I just saw leaving?"

Honestly, William didn't know. For all he knew, it could have been Thomas. "Uh, yeah. He picked me up at the foot of the mountain and offered to bring me here."

"And he didn't think to say hello? I'll have to speak to my sister. That boy!"

CHAPTER SIX

As he crossed the house's threshold, William's head swirled. The smell was overwhelming. It was the same smell he remembered from visiting his grandmother growing up. There was a cast-iron woodburning stove in the corner of the kitchen area and a stone fireplace immediately to the right of it. Both were lit and contributed to the warm, welcoming scent that reminded him of home. This only lent itself to the blurring of lines as the conflict continued in his soul between what William thought and Noah felt. The deeper William went into this predicament, the more Noah fought to come out.

William didn't know what to think about this because he was still having trouble seeing himself as Noah. If all of this were true, why couldn't he remember anything about Noah's past? It wasn't just a strange demon's twisted ploy. This was his past life. He just couldn't remember any of it. Although it seemed like his heart remembered and was fighting to let him know about it.

Mildred worked in the kitchen to prepare a meal for them, and William found himself sitting at a small, rectangular wooden table right outside the kitchen area. He was seated on a long wooden bench that looked homemade, and it felt like it as well. When William shifted slightly, the entire bench wobbled more than it should have, and he wondered if he would cause it to break. He refreshed himself with drinking well water from a jug that Mildred brought in, and he couldn't get over how fresh the water tasted, despite its slightly cloudy appearance. Growing up, he'd drunk his fill of creek and river water, which almost always had a brownish hue. It never tasted this good, though.

"I still have all your old things, your clothes, all that stuff," Mildred said as she worked in the kitchen. "After you eat a bit, you should change out of that uniform. Won't be much need for it anymore."

Nothing would please him more than to be rid of the itchy, stiff uniform.

She continued and filled him in on various things from the number of eggs she'd gathered from the hens that day to her opinion on whether the hog out in the stall was ready to be slaughtered or not. It seemed like the outside world didn't exist to her. Her world revolved around where she was and the many chores she had to do every day just to survive. She didn't even seem interested in finding out what had happened to her son in the war. She just seemed glad to have him home, and that was all that mattered.

When she brought out a hot pan of cornbread, William thought he'd ask about Liv. "Hey, Ma, Thomas told me there were some new folks that moved in around the caves after I left. Do you know where those people went when the soldiers took over?"

Mildred smiled and said, "Let's say grace."

William shook his head and folded his hands to mirror what Mildred was doing. After she said a simple prayer of thanks for the food on the table and a joyful thanks for her son coming home, she ended with an amen.

"Amen," William said, not wanting to seem rude.

As she cut the cornbread, Mildred said, "I've been helping out a few. More like they are helping me, in all honesty. With you gone and your pa passed away, I needed all the help I could get. A nice family stays out in the barn at night and helps 'round the place in the day."

He opened his mouth to ask more about that when there was a knock at the door. The knock was a sharp rap of authority against wood, and Mildred's head snapped toward the sound, her eyes narrowing with practiced suspicion.

"Round here, only trouble knocks like that. Can you see to the door, Noah?"

William went to the door and opened it to reveal an extremely old, slender Union soldier wearing a navy-blue slouch hat and a familiar face.

"You!"

There in front of him was a slightly younger but still very old Ivan.

Ivan pulled his hat off and said, "Mr. Wheaton, my name is Captain Sacks. May I trouble you for a few moments of your time? I know you were just reunited with your sweet mother here, but it will only take a moment."

William went out and pulled the door shut behind him. He noticed five Union soldiers out on the lawn accompanying their captain. One of them was holding the reins of a horse that appeared to belong to Ivan. Keeping his voice low, William said, "What the hell, Ivan? I'm spinning my wheels here. Can't you just tell me where to find Liv?"

"You're closer than you might think," Ivan said as he placed his hat back on his head. "You got to the right house all on your own, didn't you?"

Ivan pulled a cigar out of his coat side pocket, and William noticed it was not lit. He'd half expected it to be. The demon smelled it and then put it into his mouth.

"All I care about is finding Liv and getting back to my own time. I don't care about any of this."

"When you lived this life before, the first go around, you and Liv met and fell in love. You don't have to go looking for her; you'll meet at the right time. And I've dropped you in the right time, right before you meet. If you keep asking around about her, pressing these good folk, you might change things in a bad way that may not end too well for you."

"You said before that you've been influencing my life and my wife's life so that things play out the way you want them to. Even how we meet. When we meet."

"Your point?"

"So, it's okay for you to go around altering time and events but not me?"

"There's only one event you're here to alter, and that's to make sure Liv doesn't die."

"You gotta give me something. When do we meet? How long from now?"

"Not long. Just let it play out," the demon said with a wink.

"If I let it play out, she will die. I can't let that happen."

Ivan tapped William on the chest with his finger. "That's right. If you stop her from dying, that would make all of this very interesting. Very interesting indeed." With that, Ivan turned and walked toward the soldier who held his horse. He climbed on and said, "Go back inside and spend some time with your mama. She's been through enough, and she deserves to spend some time with her boy. I'll be watching you, Mr. Wheaton!"

William stood there, shaking his head, watching Ivan ride away with his squad of soldiers following behind on foot. "Would it be too much to allow his soldiers to ride horses as well? Or at least a wagon. Geez."

As he turned to go back into the house, he glanced over at the well, and there, drawing water, was a brown-haired young woman. His heart stopped. It was her. He'd know her anywhere and apparently in any time. It felt like electricity was flowing through him from head to toe. Her hair was different, but it was her. He couldn't contain himself as he took off toward the unsuspecting woman.

"Liv!"

The woman turned and looked startled at William running toward her. She dropped the water bucket, which splashed as it hit the water below.

"I found you! I thought I'd never find you!" William pulled her into his arms, but the young woman was tense.

"I'm sorry, sir. I—I'm afraid you might have mistaken me for someone else."

William heard Mildred come rushing out. "What's going on out here? I heard a shout!" Seeing William at the well, she calmed. "Noah, what did Captain Sacks want? Is everything all right?"

Not taking his eyes off the young woman in front of him, he said, "Everything's fine, Ma. He just wanted to welcome me home." William smiled his first real smile since before the car accident.

"Is that so?" Mildred said as she approached them. "Be careful of Captain Sacks, son. There's somethin' off about him." There was an edge to her voice as she issued the warning.

"Oh, you don't know how right you are," William said.

Mildred squinted at her son and wiped her hands on her apron. "I see you met Anne Jackson. Anne, this here is my son, Noah. He's just home from the war." Her voice betrayed her emotions as she choked back tears. "We thought he didn't make it, but the good Lord saw fit to bless us and bring him home."

"Yes, ma'am, uh, I mean Ms. Mildred. Sorry . . . Mildred," Anne said. "I know you said to call you by your given name; it just takes some getting used to. The way I was brought up and all." Anne smiled at Mildred, and William could tell there was a bond there.

Anne looked at William and said, "I've heard a lot about you from your ma. I feel like I already know you and everything. It's a pleasure to meet you, sir. Especially now that you're not dead and all." She looked embarrassed as she said that but as beautiful as the day William had first met her. Her brown eyes glimmered in the sun, and it reminded William of how Liv had died in his timeline.

"It's amazing how you look nearly the same! Hair and eyes are different but still the same!" William blurted out. As soon as he said it, he regretted it. This girl didn't know him. She had no memory of their life together over 150 years from now. William decided the best defense was to change the subject. "You dropped your water bucket in the well. Let me get it for you."

"No, really, there's no need to trouble yourself."

William moved to the well and looked over the lip into the darkness. Looking around, he didn't see a handle for a crank and was feeling a bit embarrassed as he realized he didn't know how to get the bucket out of the well.

"Noah! What in Sam Hill are you doing? Just use the rope, son!" She pointed at the rope hanging over the lip of the well, where it was tied to a metal anchor. With that, she turned and went back into the house, shaking her head and mumbling to herself.

Taking a step back, full of embarrassment, William took the rope and gave it a hard pull. The bucket resisted at first but then shot upward faster than he expected. Startled, he pulled harder, overcompensating, and as the bucket reached the top, it tilted, spilling water over the lip of the well. Cold water drenched his front from collar to boots. William gasped as the unexpected icy bath froze him in place for a moment. He was afraid to look at Anne, worried about how much of a fool he had just made of himself. When he finally forced himself to turn and glance over at her, she had one hand clamped over her mouth, and her eyes danced with amusement. Finally, she let out a soft chuckle.

Anne crossed her arms and tilted her head, clearly amused. "I suppose chivalry ain't dead, but it sure is a little . . . wet." She shook her head and laughed. "I appreciate the effort, truly, but next time, maybe figure out how a well works before you go playing the hero." Her teasing grin softened. "Still, it was sweet of you to try."

William was half relieved she wasn't mocking him too harshly and fully comforted that her reaction was exactly how Liv would have responded. The latter gave him hope.

"Yeah, I guess. I just wanted to help. Seeing I scared you and made you drop it in the first place. Sorry about that, about scaring you before." He rubbed his hands down the front of his uniform jacket to squeeze some water out. He then looked up and smiled at the young woman in front of him.

He remembered Mildred had said a family from the caves was staying in the barn. It must be Anne's family. "You and your family are staying in our barn?"

"Your ma, she's been such a blessing to us. My ma, pa, and little brother. We were working the caves for niter during the war, you know, over in Green Cove. Doing our part to help. The soldiers came in and took over the caves and made us leave around 'bout last winter. We had built a small place near the caves, but they said they were confiscating it and sent us on our way. Said we were lucky they didn't shoot us and burn our house to the ground. Your ma lets us stay in y'all's barn in exchange for helping out around here. When it's cold, we take shelter in the house. But we don't want to impose."

William couldn't believe his luck. He had been worried about finding Liv in a strange place and a strange time, but she was right there, standing in front of him. He wanted to hold her and kiss her. It was the first time he had seen her since the car had gone off the cliff. They both just stood there, looking into each other's eyes, and he could sense his Liv was in there; she saw him. He could tell Anne felt it too. He smiled at her, and she smiled back. He wished time would stand still. Maybe there was a silver lining in all of this. He was experiencing falling in love with her all over again.

"Anne! What's taking so long?" A boy about ten or eleven years old called out to her from beyond the garden. William could see a barn at the end of the path where the boy stood. There was another fence to the right of the path with goats and pigs contained within it. The farm was bigger than it first appeared.

"Sorry, John. Tell Ma and Pa I'll be right there." Anne turned back to William and said, "Sorry, I have to go. I'll see you 'round tomorrow, Mr. Wheaton." She tested his name as if she were trying it on for size.

"Will . . . er . . . Noah. Call me Noah," William said.

Anne took a step back and said, "Just like your ma. All right, Noah." She smiled and then turned to walk back toward the barn. William watched her the entire way. She turned back to look at him no less than a few times, her smile still not relenting. Once she was back in the barn, William turned to go back into the house.

"Still got it, McCoy. You still got it," he said to himself as he smiled ear to ear.

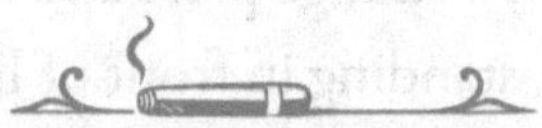

After he'd found some of Noah's old clothes and gotten out of the itchy and wet uniform, William returned to the table, where he found Mildred. She was eating more of the cornbread as he joined her. "She's a nice girl, son," Mildred said.

"I think so too." William smiled. He felt lighter, like a ton of weight had been lifted off his shoulders. The fresh clothes were still crude, but they were softer and helped him relax. He felt like things might actually work out.

"War has a way of taking more than just lives," Mildred said as she watched her son break off a piece of cornbread. "It takes peace of mind too. I've seen many a soldier return from the war with troubles, enough of my fair share to know when one's carrying a storm inside 'em. You had a brewing storm in you since the moment Thomas dropped you off."

William looked at Mildred, wondering where she was going with this.

"But there's somethin' different with you than with those other soldiers. It ain't the same kind of storm. You look like my boy. You even have his eyes."

William found himself frozen, unable to move as his mouth fell open.

She looked at him, still chewing. "I know Noah's in there; I see enough of him peeking out." Mildred pointed at William and said, "But you . . . you ain't him. So, tell me the truth. Who, or what, exactly are you?"

CHAPTER SEVEN

"That's the honest truth," William said. He had told Mildred the entire story. About Ivan, his eyes, his deal. Everything. "That's my wife out there in that barn. She's in danger, and I need to keep her alive."

Immediately, he regretted revealing everything. He didn't know how Mildred would respond. After all, if he were in her shoes, he wouldn't believe a word he had just said. It was hard for him to believe it himself even now. Maybe he should have held back a few of the more irrational points. But what part wasn't irrational?

His stomach tied in knots as Mildred pushed herself up from the chair. The sun was completely set, and darkness had crept in around them. She moved as if by memory and lit a few of the lanterns around the room. Despite his anxiety and self-awareness of how ludicrous his story sounded, he felt at peace in the dimly lit house. The smell was soothing, reminding him of his childhood.

As Mildred finished with the lanterns in the main living area, she made her way back to the table and said, "I'm half Cherokee. My father told me stories when I was little, legends and traditions of our people."

"Legends?" William leaned in against the worn table.

"Uh-huh. One particular tale I always thought was meant to keep a youngin' respectful of the world's darker corners . . ." Mildred's voice lowered, and she leaned in as if imparting a secret that might be overheard if not careful. "Untsaiyi, they called it. The red-eyed devil. A gambler who played for the highest stakes: the souls of men."

"Untsaiyi?" William said, but his attempt at pronouncing it didn't quite sound the same. "That's a word in Cherokee?"

"Yes. He is extremely evil, the embodiment of it." Mildred leaned back. "Ivan ain't just some slick-talking charlatan. From what you told me, and if my gut's worth anything at all, Ivan's workin' a plan to collect on whatever dark bargain's been struck. Now, it makes sense why Captain Sacks has always given me worry."

"Knowing what Ivan has put me and Liv through, there's nothing I'd like more than to see him dead. He said that I made a deal with him a long time ago that started all of this. I don't know what he's talking about. I don't remember making any deal with any demons."

Mildred's face softened. "I am very grateful to see the face of my boy, but I would very much like to speak with him as well. I reckon the only way that's gonna happen is if you save Anne. You have to be very careful if you want to beat the Untsaiyi. He is known as a tricky creature, and he always cheats. Even if he seems like he is on your side, he's not. None of the stories end with anyone ever beating him."

"I'm not sure how I'm supposed to save Anne. I'm reliving all of this without my memories, without Noah's memories. I just want my wife back and to be in my own time. It's taking everything I have to not run out to that barn and not leave her side for a second, but what if that ruins things for Noah and Anne, for you even? Ivan, Captain Sacks, he said I should let things play out in their natural course. But if he's this gambler you mentioned, I know I can't trust him."

"No, you can't. That's for sure," Mildred said as a tear ran down her cheek. "But I think if you succeed, my Noah will return."

"In a sense, I am Noah. I was him in this life, though it was my past life. It makes my head hurt to try and understand it." He saw a desperate mother in front of him, and his heart broke for her. "But, yes, I think he will be back as soon as I can stop Anne from dying."

Mildred smiled and wiped her cheek. She pointed to the back corner of the room. "Better keep the shotgun with you. It's already loaded. Under the floorboards there."

"Shotgun? I don't think that will work on Ivan. He can just disappear into thin air."

"Not for the devil, for Anne's protection. You don't know what is meant to take her life. You have to win. For Noah, for Anne, for your wife, and for you. For all of us." Mildred's voice was calm but commanding. She was a strong Southern woman who looked as sweet as molasses on the surface but was a hurricane underneath. This was not someone he wanted to mess with. She wanted her son back completely.

"I'm not sure how long it took Noah and Anne to fall in love, but if it was anything like it was for Liv and me, it was fast. We hit it off from the first sight."

"Oh, honey. You know as well as I do that it was the same way today," Mildred said as she reached for William's cheek but pulled her hand away. "That girl is already smitten with you."

William walked to the fireplace and lightly tapped a few boards until he found a loose one. He lifted the board, and there in the hole was an antique percussion double-barrel shotgun. Well, it wasn't antique in this time. He lifted it out of the hole and looked it over. It had two hammers and two triggers, one for each barrel. He used to hunt each fall with his grandfather with a more modern shotgun. This was similar but not completely like his. However, it seemed simple enough. Pull the hammer back, aim, and fire. He didn't see any extra ammunition in the hole, so he figured he only had two shots.

Mildred watched him look over the gun and said, "I don't have any holy water on hand, but lead and gunpowder have their own kind of holiness."

As he held the shotgun, a shiver rolled down his spine, the sensation not entirely his own. Memories tugged at the edges of his consciousness. Clouded images of damp earth, the echo of rifle fire, and the weight of chains that had bound flesh but not spirit. Noah's memories. They flooded in like a wave, and William felt the past clawing at him, demanding to be felt, to be remembered. The scent of rosemary filled his nostrils all at once.

"Rosemary!" William said. "You gave me, I mean Noah, a rosemary wreath as he was leaving for war."

"Noah! You are in there!" Her face lit up with such joy.

William rushed to his shoulder bag and opened it. There, at the bottom, was the small wreath. It was tattered but whole. The smell was faint but still there. He walked over to Mildred and smiled. "Ivan said he couldn't unlock Noah's memories for me. Said he didn't know how. I don't know how this is possible. I can't explain it, but holding that gun caused Noah's memories from the war to come through. I remember Noah's entire time after leaving to fight! Noah is coming home, I promise." He handed her the wreath and kissed her on the cheek.

Later that night, as William lay in Noah's bed trying to sleep, his mind raced. Staring at the ceiling, he tried to find peace in the familiar, but Noah's memories were like a stormy sea refusing to be stilled. It wasn't just a memory flash he'd experienced. It felt like he'd just lived through the entire ordeal. He didn't want to worry Mildred, so he didn't tell her everything. Noah had not only been captured at the Battle of Chattanooga, he had nearly died.

About a month after being put into the prisoner-of-war camp, the camp had an outbreak of measles. Noah came down with it and was transferred to a medical camp in northern Kentucky on the Ohio state line. His case was so severe he was the last of the infected to recover. This left his body weakened to the point of barely being able to move without assistance. His entire back, chest, and stomach were riddled with scars even now. Months later, once he was well enough to walk on his own, the war was over, and he was taken north, across the Ohio River, dropped off, and told he was free to make his way home the best he could. His escorts had laughed as they rode off, likely assuming they were leaving him for dead.

William felt in his gut the reality of the memories, and he was as certain he'd lived them as he was certain he hadn't. He'd felt the fear and adrenaline as he fought as a soldier and could remember the smell of the gunpowder of the rifle as he pulled the trigger. Still lingering was the determination to survive and make it home as a prisoner, the pain from the sickness, and the anger of being left for dead. He'd felt the sorrow of leaving Mildred to go to war but also the excitement at the same time. The sense of duty. Yet he also still felt like he was over a hundred years removed from all of it.

"I can't tell where he ends and I begin," William murmured to himself. The thought was insane. This wasn't just a role to play; it was a life to live. His life, Noah's life, inseparable and intertwined. His actions would affect Noah after this task was done. The responsibility weighed on him.

If he succeeded, not only would he and Liv get to continue together but so would Noah and Anne. After what Noah had been through, he deserved it.

His body finally conceded the fight to stay awake against a wall of exhaustion, and he sunk into the bed as if it were a soft grave.

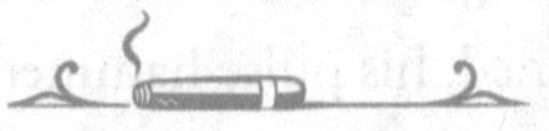

William's eyes shot open. It was dark and still nighttime. He couldn't tell what time it was exactly, but it didn't look like the sun would show its face for a while. William missed having a glowing clock beside his bed to tell him the time. He also had to fight the urge to reach for his phone.

On the window that hung beside his bed, he noticed moisture gathering on the glass. The windowpane was cool to the touch. It was a single pane of glass and offered very little protection from the chilly night air, but it was bearable. The blankets on his bed seemed to be stitched together from old clothing. The fabric varied from strip to strip. It was warm and gave him comfort.

Suddenly, the temperature in the room dropped. The windowpane started to frost over, quickly freezing his handprint in an eerie sight. William's breath became visible as he exhaled, and alarm shot through his body. He tore the covers off to jump out of the bed, but before he could swing his feet out, he heard it.

A whisper.

Faint, like wind blowing through the trees, surrounding him on every side.

"Have you wondered how this all began?"

The words hadn't come from within the room. They hadn't been spoken aloud. They were inside his head.

William stiffened, his pulse hammering. He knew that voice. It had haunted him since the hospital room when the demon had first appeared. "How?" His voice was hoarse. "Why did we make a deal?"

A low chuckle rumbled through his thoughts.

"Oh, William. It's much worse than you could ever imagine."

His skull ached, the whisper growing louder, curling around his mind like smoke.

"I remember. I remember all of it. Would you like to hear the words you spoke when you begged me to save her?"

William clutched his head with both hands, his own thoughts distant, drowning beneath the weight of Ivan's voice. The room flickered. The walls, the bed, the floor all disappeared and reappeared rapidly, then they were gone. They were replaced by a different time, a different place; somewhere dark, somewhere ancient.

A forest.

Towering trees loomed above, their twisted branches blotting out the moonlight. The air was thick with the scent of damp earth and decaying leaves. The ground beneath him was cold, packed dirt, carved into deep, worn paths that stretched in four directions.

William knelt in the center of the crossroads, his hands dug into the dirt, his breath ragged with desperation. His clothes were torn and smelled of smoke. He wore a green tunic with a quiver holding a single arrow. Tears streaked his face as his heart burned from within. In front of him, standing just beyond the shadows, was a figure. A hooded man dressed in a dark robe who seemed to blend into the night. His grin was slow and deliberate. Undeniably Ivan.

William shook; his lips trembled as he spoke with an English accent, "I don't care what it takes. Just don't let me lose her."

The words cut through William's soul. Ivan stepped closer; his voice was like silk as smoke wrapped itself around William's past self like a noose.

"There it is," the hooded demon said as his eyes glowed red. "Not for her soul. Not for her happiness. Not even for her safety. Just to keep her. How selfish. How human."

William clutched his chest, nausea washing over him. The forest flickered, the vision fading, but the whispering did not stop. It coiled around him, tightening its grip.

"You didn't save her, William. You damned her!"

The weight of those words crushed him. The room snapped back into focus. His small, rustic bedroom. The frost-covered window. The bed beneath him. But he wasn't alone.

A breath tickled his ear. Slow. Measured.

Then a whisper that was so close it made his skin crawl. "Do you really want to know what drove you to that point? What broke you to the point of making a deal with a demon like me?"

William turned, but there was nothing there.

The smell of something burning filled the air, and the temperature in the room shot back to normal as fast as it had gotten cold. William bolted out of the bed. There was no trace of Ivan in the room. As he looked back at the bed, the door to his room burst open as Mildred flew through.

"Come on! The barn is on fire! We've got to hurry!"

William rushed out the door, following Mildred through the house and out the back door. Panic came over him as it dawned on him. Anne and her family were in that barn! Was this it? Was this how she died?

CHAPTER EIGHT

illiam ran as fast as he could toward the barn. The entire structure was engulfed in fire, and flames reached out through the slats around the barn's outer walls. His mind fixed on one thing alone: Anne. Was he too late? As thick, dark smoke poured out of the openings of the barn and roof; the stinging scent of pine mixed with the smell of burned hay clawed at his throat. All that mattered was getting to Anne, and nothing was going to get in his way.

As William came to the barn, he skidded across the dirt ground to a stop, his lungs protesting as he gasped; the smoke swallowed the air around them not helping him regain his breath. He coughed and covered his nose and mouth with his arm, frantically looking for Anne.

"Anne!" he yelled between coughs.

The crackling roar of the flames almost drowned out the shouts of the Jacksons. "Noah! Mildred! Over here!"

William turned to his left and saw Anne huddled on the ground with her mother. Her hair was thrown about and hanging over her face. She was safe and alive in her mother's embrace. The sight of her unharmed gave him peace in the middle of the chaos around them. However, it was short-lived, as William's eyes landed on Anne's father, crumpled to the ground beside Anne. The old man's chest rose and fell with shallow breaths, revealing he was alive.

"My father was hit on the head as we were running out! Ma and I had to drag him the rest of the way! John is still inside!" Tears ran down their faces as they stared helplessly at the ball of fire engulfing the barn.

Sweat beaded on William's forehead from the blaze's radiating heat. He felt the dryness in his mouth and tasted ash on his tongue. The fire seemed like it was a living thing, clawing at the world around it, and William could swear he saw Ivan's red eyes in the flames. For a moment, he hesitated. Anne was safe. This was not the moment of her death. He wanted to let things play out, but he saw the concern on Anne's face. She loved her brother, and William loved her. He looked at the barn and then back at Anne. He saw Liv looking back at him. William let out a short laugh as he thought of the look on Ivan's face when he realized William wasn't going to play the demon's game any longer.

"Shit," William said under his breath. His heart was already racing as he kicked into a sprint.

"Noah!" Anne and Mildred both screamed as William ran toward the barn. He could feel the heat beckoning him, the roar of the fire taunting him.

He leaped through what remained of the main double barn doors. A huge beam thick enough around to match his leg lay across the entranceway. That must have been what knocked Anne's father unconscious. He hurdled over it and found himself standing in an opening. The heat was more intense than he had ever felt in his life. Coughing, he ripped his sleeve off and tied it around his mouth and nose.

William's eyes watered, vision blurring as he squinted to see through the smoky haze, each breath burning in his throat.

"John!"

Looking back toward the back corners, William saw they were bright orange and fully engulfed.

"John!" William coughed uncontrollably. He fell to one knee and tried to gather his strength while struggling to find air.

To his right, in a stall not fully on fire yet, he saw movement. A large wooden barrel was turned on its top, and it looked like it was trying to tilt itself over. It started to move again but quickly stilled. William rushed over to it and pushed it over. As the container rolled away, it revealed John.

John said, "I can't see which way is out!"

"Grab hold!" William motioned to his back as he squatted. John wrapped his arms around William's neck and climbed on. He hoped he remembered the way out because everywhere he turned was nothing but flames. Willliam pushed himself up as adrenaline shot through his body. He rushed forward, forgetting about the beam in the doorway, and tripped. However, his momentum sent them both bursting forward through the flames and into the night air.

William landed face-first in the dirt, which was littered with rocks, and his cheek burned almost instantly. The metallic taste of blood came just as fast. John rolled forward, having landed on his side as they both hit the ground.

"John! Noah!" Anne and Mildred ran forward. Mildred helped John move away from the fire, and Anne knelt to help William. William noticed a few other people had arrived. "The neighbors came," Anne said. "They've started a water line."

A few of the men ran back and forth on the path from the barn to the well, bringing buckets of water, throwing it on the fire, and then hurried back up the path again. Others were using shovels to throw dirt on the flames.

Anne and William managed to get far enough away from the fire and collapsed on the ground together. Tears flowed down Anne's face. She took her hand and brushed it against his battered cheek with a tenderness that made his body numb.

"Thank you, Noah. I don't know how to repay you. John means everything to us. We would have been devastated without him!"

There was something more than gratefulness in her gaze. It was an expression he recognized. William smiled but grimaced from the pain of doing so.

"Honestly, I think I would do it a thousand times for you."

Anne's face was already red from the heat of the fire, but he could tell he'd embarrassed her. She threw herself into his arms and wrapped her arms around him. She hid her face in his chest as William embraced her. They sat there locked together, the roar of the fire dimming around them as the chaos died away.

By midday, the fire had burned out. It, along with everything inside, was a total loss. Anne's father had come to and was lying in Mildred's bed with a wet cloth on his head. It turned out the fire started when he'd knocked over his reading lantern into a hay pile. It was so dry that once it lit, there was no stopping it. He was full of remorse and promised to rebuild the barn himself once he was healed.

"Over my dead body, Mr. Jackson!" Mildred said. "I'm just glad y'all are alive and all right!"

William grunted, rubbing the stiffness from his limbs. The left side of his face was swollen with a mixture of red and purple. His lip was cut, and his left eye had a black ring under it. He stood, ignoring the cry of his muscles, and cast a glance toward Anne, who was tying her hair up with a ribbon.

"Captain Sacks won't be an easy man to sway," Anne said, her hair catching the sunlight as it came through the window. "But we have to try and convince him to give us our place back. The Union has been returning property and land to the original owners as of late. We've been putting off asking because of the caves. I'm sure with them being on our land, it might not be a simple request, but it seems we have no choice but to ask now."

Mildred nodded, looking at William with a knowing glance. "With a few stipulations, I'm sure," she said.

"Without a doubt," William said, the good corner of his mouth twitching upward. "Though I might have an in with the good captain."

"None of that!" Mildred said. "You know what he is, Noah! Captain Sacks isn't one to play around with! There will be a price to pay! Don't you think we've all paid enough to that devil already?"

"I have to try," William said. His tone was respectful. "You know why. I can't let her go alone."

"What's all this about?" Anne said, though her playful smirk showed no real objection to the offered help or accompaniment. "We don't want to be any trouble. Trouble's been following my family since the day the first Union soldier set foot in the South."

"Trouble might think it can claim squatter's rights, but it's got another think coming, dear," Mildred said. "Son, take the gun. If you want to end this, you'll need to be more cunning than the devil you're up against. This ain't no game."

William and Anne decided to go into town the next day to speak with Captain Sacks.

"I am not sure he'll even listen to us," Anne said, breaking the quiet as they made their preparations.

"Only one way to find out." William's body ached with every movement, but he didn't want to be anywhere else as long as Anne was there by his side. "We go in there, hat in hand if we must, but we don't leave until we get your family's land back."

"Or until they throw us out on our asses." Anne seemed to surprise herself with her use of that word, and a smile lit up her face.

"Damn, Miss Jackson, you kiss your mother with that mouth?"

"Only when necessary."

William's heart pounded. He loved her. No matter what lifetime it was. He leaned forward to kiss her, but she put her hand up and caught his chin.

"Hold on, Mr. Wheaton," she said with a playful smile. "You have to be careful there with your wounds." She looked intently at his lips, studying them, and then kissed the unharmed corner of his mouth. "That's all for now, sir. You have to make an honest woman of me if you want more of that."

CHAPTER NINE

The next morning, William and Anne set out for the town William had passed through with Thomas a few days prior. They rode on Mildred's flatbed wagon, drawn by her mule, Quincy, who Mildred said was just as stubborn as he looked. However, they had no issues with him as they started their journey. It was the most pleasant wagon ride William had yet to experience. No disrespect to Thomas, but Anne made for better company.

"Why do I feel like I've known you my entire life, Noah? We met only two days ago."

William understood. It was the same feeling both he and Liv had had the day they met each other in college. He didn't understand it then, but after all of this, he did now. He still didn't understand how it was possible, but he understood the concept.

"I know what you mean. I feel the same way." William was also getting the picture that things in this time period didn't work the same way they did in the modern world. He wanted to lean over and kiss Anne, but she had made it clear that would be considered inappropriate. "I don't know what to do," he said, looking at her. "I want to hold your hand,

I want to kiss you, and I'm telling the truth . . . I'm gonna marry you. But I don't know the proper way to do that here. Do I ask your dad for permission first? I'm not sure what is okay."

"You are very forward, sir!" She laughed. "I think we should probably keep our focus on the task at hand. There will be plenty of time to talk about all of that properly once we have my family's land back."

William smirked. Smiling was still too painful. Even now, she was the levelheaded one who kept him focused. He snapped the reins. "Quincy! Let's go! We gotta get there and back as fast as possible!"

Quincy didn't speed up or slow down. He just kept to his steady pace and twitched his ear.

William snapped the reins again, to no effect.

Anne leaned over and kissed William on his cheek, which happened to be the side not injured and bruised by his heroic feat. "You won't get that stubborn mule to move faster than he wants to. Quincy will get us there in due time. Let's just enjoy the morning and each other's company."

William didn't know how to tell Anne her time was short if he couldn't find a way to save her. She would meet the same fate as Liv had in his own time. Remembering how Liv had died, he thought it best Quincy did take his sweet time. If the wagon wrecked at the speed they were creeping along, only a few scratches would come of it. So, he sat back and took Anne's advice.

About midmorning, they arrived at a building in town Anne directed them to. It seemed to be a popular establishment, with a dozen or so people going in and out. A few Union soldiers stood out front with rifles. One soldier was seated at a table, wearing a pistol at his side. His uniform resembled Ivan's from the other day and had different markings from the others. William wasn't sure how to read the ranks on the soldier's shoulder and didn't know how to address him. He was clearly an officer, but he didn't want to insult the man by calling him the wrong rank.

"Excuse me, sir. Can you direct us to Captain Sacks?"

The officer looked at William and then at Anne. "Are you talking to me, boy?"

Anne stepped forward. "We're sorry, Lieutenant. Mr. Wheaton here has just returned. We mean no disrespect."

The lieutenant looked at Anne, and his demeanor softened. He glanced back over to William with suspicious eyes. "What's your business with Captain Sacks, Miss?"

"We wish to speak to him and petition for the return of my family's land and house due to hardship. It's in Green Cove, near the caves."

The lieutenant stiffened when Anne mentioned the caves. "I'm not sure that will be possible, Miss. The caves are still off-limits."

"Please, Lieutenant, we understand President Johnson is allowing confiscated land to be returned to the original landowners. My family just lost everything in a fire, and we have no place to stay."

Anne seemed very polite and patient. More so than William wanted to be or would be if he were speaking.

The lieutenant seemed not to want to be bothered with this and turned to look inside the building. He turned back to William and Anne with a smirk on his face. William guessed he had some sort of dislike for the good captain. "Go on in. Captain Sacks is in the very back."

William and Anne made their way through the door, and William noticed it was the town's general store, with food items and various other necessities lying around on shelves. It was busy, with several customers milling around the store and one paying for a purchase. The pair walked the center aisle, which led to the back of the store, where there was a lone door on the back wall.

William looked at Anne and said, "I suppose we knock?"

Knocking on the door was followed by a muffled, "Come," from the other side. As they walked through the door, they were met with a cloud of cigar smoke. Anne coughed and waved her hand in front of her face. "Welcome! So nice to see you both." The voice unmistakably belonged to Ivan. "What can I do for you today?"

Anne, taking charge, spoke first. "Captain Sacks, my family's home and land were confiscated during the war. We've been living at the home of Mr. Wheaton here, and we recently lost everything in a fire. I'd like to petition for the release of our home and land back to my family so we can rebuild our lives. We, like so many others, are grateful the war is finally over and our great country is finally together in one union once again."

William was amazed. Anne was well-spoken and quite shrewd. If Captain Sacks wasn't actually the devil in the flesh, it might have worked to shine light on the union of the country and distaste for the war.

"Miss, uh, what did you say your last name was?"

"Oh, pardon me, sir. I didn't say. However, my full name is Anne Olivia Jackson."

"Olivia?" William said.

Anne looked over and smiled. "Why, yes, Mr. Wheaton. I was given that name in honor of my great-grandmother."

Ivan interrupted. "Where did you say your home and land were located, Miss Jackson?"

"In Green Cove, sir." Anne left out the location of the caves. It seemed she'd picked up on the lieutenant's reaction to that piece of information before.

Ivan's smile had never left his face since they'd walked in. It was as if he was enjoying this a bit too much. It was obvious to William he was playing with them. "Isn't that near the caves, ma'am?"

"Why, um, yes, sir. It is. However, my family has no interest in the caves. We only wish to occupy the homestead and work the land around it. You have my word."

"The word of a rebel is not worth much here, Miss. With all due respect and all. You have to see this from my perspective. Those caves were used to produce gunpowder that was then used to kill Union, better said, American lives. I would need assurances from your family . . ." Ivan then looked at William. ". . . and Mr. Wheaton, here, that the caves would remain untouched and unused."

"What kind of assurances?" William said. No pleasantries, no titles. Just straight to the point. Perhaps a bit of PTSD from dealing with this demon already.

"I'm glad you asked, Mr. Wheaton," Ivan said, not letting his smile slip for a second. "It's quite simple, really. The only issue that needs to be resolved pertaining to Ms. Jackson's homestead is the matter of the caves. That gunpowder was used to butcher so many during the war. We simply cannot allow them to be accessed freely."

Anne inserted herself and said, "Yes, sir, we completely understand. You have my word. My family's word. We will not enter the caves. We will even act as custodians to protect them and not allow others entry as well."

"I'm afraid that is not enough, Ms. Jackson."

"What would you have us do then?" William said.

"We've already tried to blast the caves to seal them off with black powder but no luck. The rock is too stubborn," Ivan said, pulling a fresh cigar from his uniform's inside pocket. He sniffed the side and put the cigar in his mouth while he continued, "There is this new stuff from Europe. Germany, I think. Invented by some guy named Nobel. Calls it nitroglycerin."

"Dynamite!" William said.

Ivan put a match to his cigar and took some puffs. "Yes. That's right. New stuff, very unstable, though. It leveled a bank building out in San Francisco last year, killing over a dozen people. It even damaged the surrounding buildings for a couple of city blocks!"

William was getting nervous. Where was Ivan headed with this? William certainly didn't want anything to do with dynamite. The stuff was so unstable that the slightest jolt would set it off.

"How does this involve us?" William said.

"My boy, you are the ones asking for the land those caves sit on to be returned. That's my price. I was going to send some men down to the caves today, but now that you've presented this opportunity, I don't have to risk losing any men. Good help is so hard to find! My men will load your wagon with enough crates of the stuff for you to blow the mouth of each cave. There are two. We will give you four crates. A couple of crates in each entrance should get the job done."

William stood. "It's too dangerous. We won't do it."

Anne stood as well and directed her gaze at William. "I don't think we have a choice. This is my family's home. I don't know anything about this nitro . . . dyno . . ."

"Dynamite," William helped her. "I know about this stuff. It's dangerous and has been known to blow up just from bumping it. A small amount is enough to kill everyone around it for several yards. The amount he is talking about could level a full city block in seconds. I don't want you to get hurt."

"I understand it's dangerous. I do. And I can tell you care about me, and to be honest, I have the same feelings toward you. But if you would let me finish what I was saying. If we are to be together, I need to know my family is safe and secure in their own home once again. Perhaps we can hire some hands to move the crates, and then Captain Sacks's men can make the explosion happen . . ."

"I'm afraid not, Miss," Ivan said. "Like I said, I don't want to risk my men. This is the deal, I'm afraid. You must take the crates to the caves and set them off by sundown today if you want the homestead back. I don't care if Mr. Wheaton joins you or not, but as a gentleman, I am certain he will accompany you."

"Why the urgency? Why does this have to be done today?" William said.

"There's been an order from the state capital to auction off any seized land that has not been claimed by the previous owners. The order goes into effect tomorrow morning." Ivan puffed on his cigar and blew out a cloud of smoke. "My hands are tied. You have until the end of the day to reclaim your land, and since by all accounts, we know the Jackson family was personally involved in using the caves to make weapons, I cannot in good conscience allow you to take possession of the homestead unless the caves are sealed. It's your choice, of course. You can always bid on the place tomorrow, though you'll still be required to seal the caves before you take possession. Either way, dynamite is in this picture."

William saw a way to delay this craziness and save Anne. He could keep her away from the explosion. "But by waiting and winning the auction tomorrow, we could take our time and hire hands to help with the sealing of the caves, no?"

Ivan shook his head slowly, pulling his cigar from his mouth. "I suppose so, yes. But there is no guarantee you will win the auction. I know for a fact there are several people interested in the place. It's good land, good for farming and raising stock . . . and a family." Ivan winked at William.

"Noah," Anne said. "Please, we can do this. My father doesn't have any money. He spent everything we had when he purchased the land when we arrived here. We can't win at the auction."

"Perhaps Mildred . . . uh . . . my mother, perhaps she can help. I'm sure she has enough."

"She doesn't. Since you've been gone, she's used everything she had to help people in need around here. Most people here have lost everything during the war."

William turned to Ivan. "If that's true, who would have enough money to bid on the land and the house?"

Ivan was smiling again, and William thought he saw his eyes glimmer red for half a second. "Several of the soldiers have fallen in love with this small mountain community. I, myself, have even been tempted to settle here. It's nice." Ivan put the shortened cigar back in his mouth and leaned back in his chair.

William wanted to punch the pompous demon. He couldn't move supernaturally fast or disappear with Anne here. Not without giving himself away. William clenched his fists and was about to make a move toward Ivan when Anne grabbed his arm. She looked from Ivan to William. "It's okay, Noah. It's early still. We can take the crates to the caves today." She pulled William's arm to go but stopped. "How do we make the dynamite explode once the crates are in place?"

"I believe your soon-to-be husband knows how to accomplish that, my dear." Ivan stood and smiled. "Might I also add a congratulations on the pending nuptials? So you are aware, I also have the power to perform a marriage ceremony as magistrate of this county."

"Not in your wildest dreams," William said. His patience was wearing thin, and his anger for this devil boiled. Anne saw it and thanked Ivan. She hooked her arm into William's and led him out of the office into the store area. She had to use a little force to get William to move.

"This is too dangerous. We can build your family their own place on my mother's land. I'm sure of it. In the place of the barn. Perhaps that's why God allowed it to burn. To help keep you safe."

"I don't know if I want much more of the Almighty's help if He tends to keep His sheep safe by throwing them into a fire!" Anne smiled. "I know we just met and all, and we are still getting to know each other. I, for one, might not be very good at understanding you as of yet, but please understand: that home is important to me. My father built it himself. It's a beautiful place. The whole cove glows the most vibrant colors every morning as the sun rises and then again in the evening as the sun slides behind the mountains.

There's a cool creek running through the meadow, and the land is good for crops and for feeding cattle. My father said it's the place he has been dreaming of his entire life. His paradise. We have to save it."

The look Anne gave him he knew all too well. Liv had given it to him all the time when she wanted William to do something he didn't want any part in. It went straight to his heart. "I'll take the wagon and blow the crates. I want you to stay here or make your way back to the house. That's the only way I'll agree to do this."

"You don't know the way on your own, I'm afraid," Ivan said from behind William.

William turned around and saw Ivan wearing his captain's hat, leading eight men. Four crates were being held by two men each, one on each side of each crate. They all looked scared out of their minds. One soldier was sweating profusely. Ivan turned and pointed to the wagon. "Over there, load it on that wagon. Don't move too quickly."

"Geez! Are you crazy?"

"Maybe," Ivan said, smiling. "Look, son, Ms. Jackson, here, will need to ride with you. You don't know the way." He leaned in and whispered, "Noah would know the way, but you don't, William."

William answered in a normal volume, not caring anymore, "I'll find Thomas. He'll know the way."

Ivan shook his head. "Not enough time. As it is, it's already ten, and by the time you get to the cove and get the crates unloaded, you'll just make it." He leaned in close again. "Wagons don't move as fast as cars, son. Things take a bit longer in this day and time."

William looked around. It didn't appear that anyone on the street was paying any attention. He hoped someone would speak up or overhear. Then Southern hospitality would assert itself and people would offer to help with this task. It seemed people tried very hard to steer clear of Captain Sacks on purpose.

"I don't get it," William said. "You said this was a chance to save Anne and, in turn, save Liv. You said you were bored and wanted to change things. How can I save her if you won't allow me to keep her away from this? This is how she dies, isn't it?"

"I don't recall saying it would be easy. Do you?" Ivan stood straight. "That's the deal, Mr. Wheaton. You take Ms. Jackson with you and seal the caves tight. My men will hear the explosion and make their way there to confirm before sunset. If you can take care of this by then, I give you my word, the deed to the homestead will belong to Ms. Jackson's family before morning."

Ivan turned and went into the store. William looked at the wagon. "This is so very dangerous. We're going to have to go super slow so we don't accidentally set off those crates."

"Super?" Anne frowned with her eyebrows drawn.

"As slow as we can go and still get there on time." William guessed that word was not a popular term yet. Anne directed William to the path that led down the back side of the mountain and into Green Cove. William felt every pebble and dip the wagon made, all the while praying he could find a way to keep them both alive.

CHAPTER TEN

Halfway down the mountain, the road opened on the left side. William saw that it curved downward and leveled out for a bit, then continued down to the valley floor. Below where things leveled out, there was a break in the trees, and a house sat in the middle of a good-sized field. The house was made from logs, with a stone chimney on each end. William had never seen a real log cabin before. The way the mountain descended to the valley floor on three sides reminded him of a football stadium. The direction they were headed, the only side not surrounded by the mountains, seemed to be the only way to enter the valley.

"Beautiful, isn't it?" Anne said. "It took my father all spring and most of a summer to clear the area and get the house built. He used the trees he cleared as lumber for the house."

"This is Green Cove?"

"Why, yes. In the spring and summer the trees are as green as can be. We assumed that's where the name comes from, but we're not certain. It was named before we arrived." Anne tilted her head and smirked. "Why are you pretending not to know about this place? You were raised here, and your mother told us you used to disappear down in here hunting with your pa."

William didn't know how to answer her and not sound crazy. He was sure she would not be as receptive as Mildred had been. So, he decided to be as truthful as he could. "It's a long story. I'll tell you one day, but I'm afraid now is not the best time."

Anne seemed a little disappointed. "You're not already losing interest in me, are you, Noah? I know we disagreed back in town . . ."

William smiled and looked at her and saw Liv in her eyes. "There's nothing in this universe that could make me lose interest in you. And I doubt that's the last disagreement we'll ever have. Believe me. But you're the whole reason I'm here. I'm going to save you, I promise. I'll make things right."

"Save me?" Anne looked back at the crates. "I gather that transporting these crates is dangerous, and I suppose I'll see soon enough the damage they can do, but I trust you, I do. You don't have to save me. I'm all right."

William's eyes welled up, and he reached for Anne's cheek. Anne leaned into his hand and covered his hand with her palm. She closed her eyes as he leaned in and kissed her. "I love you," he whispered.

Anne blushed. "You're using strong words, Mr. Wheaton."

William's heart sank, and he feared he had made a mistake. To his surprise, Anne put her arm around his and scooted closer to him on the seat.

"But it's exactly how I feel as well. I love you too. That's exactly the best way to describe how I've felt since we met." Anne laughed. "It's like a story from a book, love at first sight. It's every little girl's fantasy." She looked at him with an assuring aura. "That's what it is, though. True love finding its home."

As they reached the valley, a smaller road led toward the house, and Anne directed William toward it. They made their way through, and William noticed there were heavy wagon tracks that formed deep ruts as they went along. It was rough, and the wagon bounced more than he was comfortable with.

"We're going to have to go even slower, I'm afraid. If we hit a pothole or a rock or something, we won't make it to the caves."

"The road certainly is rougher than I remember. There must have been a lot of back-and-forth through here since we were forced out."

"When did your family leave? This all must be from transporting the saltpeter during the war."

"No, there's another road going along the foot of the mountain for that. It is covered by the tree canopy, so loads could be taken out without being seen. The soldiers must have used this route. We left here last winter, when the soldiers first came. A Colonel Streight took control of the caves and left Captain Sacks in charge, while he went on to fight elsewhere."

When they arrived at the house, William stopped the wagon and saw an opportunity. "How about you stay here while I put the crates in place and set them off? You got us this far, and we shouldn't tempt fate more than we have to. We're not out of danger yet, and I'd feel much better if you were not anywhere close to this stuff when it goes off."

"Those crates look heavy. It took two soldiers to load each of them; I think I might need to help you unload them. If they are as easily startled as you say, you shouldn't try to unload them all by yourself."

She was right, of course. Liv was always right, even in a previous life. He couldn't risk it, though. He had to save her.

"I can take the lids off and unload them a few at a time. Inside the crates are these long, round sticks."

William knew moving them outside of the crates was even more dangerous, and even trying to remove the crate lids could set them off. He didn't care, though, as long as Anne was safe.

Anne reluctantly agreed and got out of the wagon. William followed in order to walk her into the house. As they approached the porch, the front door opened and out came a man in worn brown clothes. He seemed to be in his mid to late thirties and, from his appearance, was a man who worked the fields for a living.

"Mr. Ryan?" Anne said with confusion.

"Ms. Jackson. What a pleasure it is to see you again. I was just passing through and was checking on the welfare of your family's place."

Moving closer to William, Anne said, "Mr. Ryan, this is Mr. Wheaton. My family has been staying at his homestead, and we are in process of getting our place back from Captain Sacks. Mr. Wheaton is here to help me with the final details."

"I see," Mr. Ryan said. "I remember your pa, Mr. Wheaton. I reckon the last I saw you, you was a bit shorter and just learning to hunt 'round here. It's mighty kind of you to help the Jacksons out during their time of need."

His smile reminded William of a used-car salesman.

Mr. Ryan looked over at the wagon and seemed to notice the crates. "What do you have there, Mr. Wheaton? I see writing on those boxes, but I don't read very well."

Anne said, "It's nothing to be concerned with, Mr. Ryan." Anne pointed toward the house. "I just wanted to check on the house while we were out this way. Does everything appear to be in order to you?"

Still eyeing the wagon, Mr. Ryan said, "Why yes, ma'am, it does." He turned his gaze to William and then back to Anne. "All in order, indeed. I should be on my way. As I said, I was just passing through." Mr. Ryan walked off the porch, passing Anne and William. "Ms. Jackson. Mr. Wheaton."

William and Anne watched Mr. Ryan as he slowly walked past the wagon. He looked closely at the contents, then walked at a normal speed down the road, the way they had just come.

"He strikes me as trouble. Did you get a whiff of him? Smelled like he's been in Thomas's moonshine."

Anne's voice was stern and had a hint of concern. "He's been asking my father for my hand in marriage ever since we arrived. He owns a good deal of land not far from here. His first wife died, I'm told, about two years before we settled here, right after the war started. He's a strict man, from what I've seen, and when he's had some drink, well, he can become unruly. I'm surprised he was so calm, considering . . ."

William walked Anne into the house, and he was amazed by the simplicity of the inside. It was just one large room. In one corner was a wooden ladder leading to a platform or loft hanging over half the room.

"John and I slept in the top, and my ma and pa stayed under here." Anne looked around, and there was sadness in her voice. "Everything is gone. We left in such a hurry, we didn't take much. From the looks of it, someone cleaned the place out."

"Probably Captain Sacks and his men."

"Hmm." Anne nodded in agreement. "Well, go on. I'll gather some wood and get a fire going. We will probably have to stay the night here. Even after Captain Sacks's men come when the explosion goes off, we shouldn't try to return up the mountain in the dark."

"Right. Which way are the caves?"

"It's not far. If it weren't for the trees, they'd be right there plain as day. Just follow the road straight ahead. The entrances are on the far end of the cove. The road will lead you to the largest one directly. There is one to the left also.

It's not far. Sound carries in the cove, so please holler when you're ready to set off the . . . what did you call it?"

"Dynamite. How loud do I need to yell?"

"Come here." Anne smiled and took William's hand. She led him out to the front porch and faced straight ahead toward the mountain. She let out a quick, "Yep!" The sound carried and bounced back with a clear echo as loud as the yell she'd just let out.

"Yep!" William smiled as his voice echoed back. "So cool."

Anne looked at him with curiosity. "I'll get the fire going for you, so it will be warm when you return."

"Oh, no. Sorry." He gave a short laugh. "I just meant the echo was cool. I mean, it was something I found some pleasure in."

"I see," Anne said with a smile. "Well, that's not something many of us have had the opportunity to find for some time. I think spending time with you, Noah, is . . . cool."

It sounded awkward and strange and a bit forced, but William smiled and kissed Anne's cheek.

"I'd better get this over with. I'll yell soon."

CHAPTER ELEVEN

William noticed the day was getting away from him as he arrived at the first cave. Ivan was right; the trip had taken longer than he'd anticipated. It was just a few miles from town and would have been only a little bit in a car, but by wagon, it took some time. The caves were not far from the cabin, but it felt like a mile with the pace William wanted to keep to not have his cargo go off prematurely.

The first cave opening was about twenty feet wide and just about as high. All around it was exposed rock that rose about fifteen feet and leveled off a bit with grass and trees sitting on top of the entrance, where the mountain rose above. A small creek came out of the mouth of the cave on one side, and a dirt path led into the cave beside it. Along the exposed rock wall ran another path going to the left. William assumed it led to the other cave.

The crates proved to be too heavy for William to lift by himself, and prying the lids off wasn't possible by hand. He needed a crowbar or something like that.

"Damn," he said to himself.

He had left the shotgun at the house with Anne, hoping it would keep something from happening to her while he was away. He looked around and walked into the mouth of the cave, hoping to find a stick or something he could use to pry the crate lid off. There was a long wooden trough along one of the cave walls that came out of the darkness of the back of the cave and ran to the opening. The remnants of some kind of operation. He didn't know the particulars of how to gather saltpeter from caves, but he knew the trough was part of that process.

Not seeing anything helpful, William turned and walked back out of the cave. He decided to try the other cave to see if anything was there he could use to open the crates.

As soon as he sat on the wagon, he heard a familiar voice. "Against my better judgment, I was trying to help you out."

The hair on the back of William's neck stood on end. "What?" William said as he turned toward the demon. "If you want to help out, you can help by getting these crates into the caves."

Ivan walked closer. He was in his original older form and dressed in his tweed suit, bowtie, and homburg hat in place. He stopped beside the wagon and put a cigar in his mouth, which lit on its own.

"Hey! Put that out! You'll set off the dynamite!" William jumped from the wagon and put himself between Ivan and the crates.

"Relax, boy! That stuff can't hurt me," Ivan said as he puffed on his cigar. "You, though, it could hurt you." Ivan laughed. "Don't worry, what fun would it be if you died now?"

That didn't make William feel any better.

Ivan looked William up and down like he was sizing him up. "I must admit to my surprise, everything you've done so far is almost exactly how it happened the first time. Noah even left Anne at the house originally. Some of Noah's mind must be seeping through into yours."

That caught William off guard. "What? Almost everything?" This caused some worry to creep in. What if he couldn't change things? He had to find a way to do things differently than Noah would. He had to slow down and think things through. "Speaking of Noah's memories coming through, earlier, I had a memory of Noah leaving for the war, and of a little wreath his mother packed for him. And then I remembered everything about the war. Everything. The strangest part was, it wasn't just remembering things; I felt it, emotions and all."

"Mmmm." Ivan squinted his eyes. "Really? That's interesting . . . and unexpected." Ivan blew out some smoke, clearly considering what he'd just been told. "I didn't say Noah's memories might be slipping through; I said his mind must be. The way he thinks. Causing you to think the same way. But then again, you are the same person when you break it down, so maybe that's not so strange. The memory, though . . . that isn't good, actually. But that explains why everything is happening almost like it did the first time."

"Why is that not good? It's hard to navigate here, not knowing where I'm going or who people are. Hell, not knowing the customs of the day has caused some issues."

"I told you before that your biggest advantage here was not having Noah's memories. I thought because of that, you'd make different choices than Noah did the first time around. But, well . . ." Ivan's face grew serious.

Ivan reached and tilted his hat back, a shadow of concern across his face. William partially got some enjoyment from seeing the demon on his heels, but at the same time, it worried him because he didn't have a way back to his own lifetime without Ivan.

"Doing stuff with past lives is delicate; even I can't predict every ripple."

"Ripple?" William's hands clenched into fists. "You said I had to save Anne, and by doing that I would save Liv. Now, you're saying what, exactly?"

"Look, kid, time isn't real. Not the way you think of it anyway. It's just something humans invented to measure and keep track of events and the duration of things. How old they are, how long it's been since their last paycheck, you get the idea."

"What the hell? Time is real. I was born, I grew, and things happened. There is a past and a present and a future."

"Well, not really. How can I explain this?" Ivan flicked his cigar to the ground. "You might like to think of life like a train. Each car of the train is a day of your life, and you're moving from car to car until you reach the end of the train and you die. You only see one car at a time, one day at a time. However, there are many trains on the track before and after yours; life happened before you, and it continues after you. Is that how you see time?"

"I've not given it that kind of thought," William said, though internally he wondered if this evil being in front of him had actually lost his mind. "But I suppose that makes sense."

"Well, forget that, that's all bullshit! It's not a long line like a train; it's more like, like a, uh . . . a pancake! Stacked on top of each other. Your life, Noah's life, Liv's life, Anne's, everyone's life. It's stacked like a pile of pancakes. Every one of your past lives, your current life, all your future lives are happening at once. Stacked on top of each other."

"Hang on. This makes no sense. If everything is happening at once, why do we only experience one 'pancake' or lifetime at a time? Or is each 'pancake' only a day or year? What about cause and effect? Does that even exist? If I punch you in the face right now, are you saying it already happened and also hasn't happened yet?"

Ivan narrowed his eyes. "Not exactly. Sometimes other lives, or timelines, for lack of a better word, bleed through. When someone sees a ghost, for example. There's no such thing as actual ghosts. When that happens, it's actually a point where two timelines are bleeding through on top of each other. You're seeing into another timeline for a moment, then it's gone. You see a ghostly figure, and they see you the same way in their timeline. Are you getting this now?"

"Uh, not really . . . sort of." William didn't know what to say.

"Your life with Liv. Noah's life with Anne. They happen at the same time. You save her here, you save Liv at the same time. Yours and Liv's lives bleed through and touch all the other lives you both have lived."

"Okay, so if that's true, how does changing something here cause a ripple?"

"If you throw a stone into a lake, when it hits the water, the ripples start flowing out from the impact point, right? You being here has caused some ripples, but because you haven't gone off the path very much from what you did when you were Noah the first time, according to your perception of time, I figured the ripples would be small. Until the big change of saving Anne, that is. But something you've done has caused a big enough ripple that allowed Noah's memories to seep through."

"I think you're nuts. Is that it? Is that why you've been torturing Liv and me? You're some kind of escapee from a demon loony bin?"

"Listen," Ivan growled, "we don't have time for your lip! Just understand, nothing is isolated. Everything you do here ripples. It has a ripple effect through every lifetime. You having Noah's memories wasn't part of the plan. No . . . "

"Wait. The other night, when you were torturing me, whispering in my head, you showed me the moment we made our deal. You were about to show me what drove me to that point in that lifetime. What happened to Liv in that life? If we hadn't made that deal, would all of this be happening? Would whatever happened then ripple through every lifetime instead?"

Ivan's lips curled up into a smile. His grin stretched, slow and satisfied, as if savoring a secret he'd been waiting to reveal. "I get a lot of joy from your suffering, my boy. I think you understand that by now. I do, in fact, show you what happened in that life every time we meet, in every lifetime right before you die and are reborn to start the cycle all over again."

"I need to know," he said. "What happened?"

Ivan let out a slow, amused chuckle, shaking his head. "Oh, William." His eyes burned into him. "It's all about what you did to her. You've spent all these lifetimes thinking you're the victim. That this curse is something I did to you. But, kid . . ." Ivan leaned in close, voice low and taunting. "You brought this on yourself."

William's skin went ice cold. "What do you mean? I would never do this to us. I wouldn't hurt her."

Ivan barked a laugh. "Oh, you already did!" His expression darkened, his voice was full of cruel delight. "You didn't just lose Liv in that first life, William. You killed her!"

"No. You're lying!" William took a step back. "I . . . would never . . ."

"But you did!" Ivan's voice dripped like venom. "You didn't do it on purpose, of course. It was an accident. You held her as the life drained from her eyes. You begged her to stay. You sobbed her name. And when you realized what you'd done . . . when guilt sank its claws into your soul, you broke."

The truth dug its way into William's chest.

Ivan's voice turned almost gentle. "That was when you called for me at the crossroads. You asked for a way out of the pain. A way to undo what couldn't really be undone. And I, being the generous soul that I am, gave you exactly what you asked for. I brought her back, and you both had one lifetime to grow old and die a peaceful death. One happy life. I must say, it was beautiful. But bringing someone back to life has a price. Death must be satisfied; it has an order that can't be changed. The cost for cheating death in that life was an eternity of death for Liv."

"If that's true, what happens if I save Anne? What happens if I save Liv at the end of all of this?"

Ivan smiled. "That's what you're about to find out, my boy."

As if right on cue, a loud scream and the crack of a gun echoed through the trees.

CHAPTER TWELVE

"**A**nne!"

The gunshot came from the direction of the cabin, echoing through the holler, making it sound like a cannon had gone off. William bolted toward the wagon, but as he was about to jump on, he looked at the crates of dynamite in the back. Thinking of how long it would take to get back to the cabin, he considered unhooking Quincy to ride but decided against it. He turned and took off with a sprint toward the cabin.

The thick pine scent of the surrounding trees filled his lungs as he shouldered past low-hanging branches, each stride bringing him closer to Anne, not knowing if he'd find her dead or alive. He finally arrived, not slowing as he ascended the porch and burst through the door. His heart hammered in his chest, adrenaline moving him forward.

"Anne!" His voice was raw, torn from a throat tight with fear.

And there she was, Anne Olivia Jackson, her brown hair a wild cascade around her gentle face, now twisted with terror and tears. Mr. Ryan had cornered her against the wall under the loft, and she was holding the shotgun level and pointed right at his head.

Mr. Ryan held a large hunting knife in his right hand and was not taking his eyes off her. Anne saw William burst in, and as she looked at him, Mr. Ryan didn't miss his opportunity. He leaped toward Anne and sliced across her shirt, causing her to drop the shotgun as she screamed.

As the gun hit the ground, Mr. Ryan kicked it out to the far corner of the room. Anne's shirt, now ripped open by the blade, revealed parted flesh and blood, turning her stomach red.

"Get away from her!" William yelled as he raced toward Anne's attacker.

Mr. Ryan's quick reflexes took William by surprise as he turned and threw his left elbow into William's face as William was about to grab him. The blow caught William on his injured cheek, which sent him backward, landing on his back. William rolled over, holding his cheek, which was now bleeding again, and tried to prop himself up to get back on his feet. He looked toward the shotgun and made a move in its direction, but Mr. Ryan rushed to him and kicked William in the gut, knocking the wind out of him.

Laughing, Mr. Ryan said, "Come on, you son of a bitch! Once I'm done with you, I'll have my way with her!"

Gasping for air, William looked over at Anne, who had fallen to the floor against the wall and was crying uncontrollably, hiding her face in her knees.

Mr. Ryan moved over to the shotgun and bent over to retrieve it when William, having gathered the strength to get to his feet, tackled him. Knowing he couldn't restrain Mr. Ryan and hold the gun long enough to shoot him, William kicked the gun toward Anne. He then grabbed Mr. Ryan's arm and slammed it on the ground while sitting on his back. Mr. Ryan held firm to the knife as William raised his arm and slammed it a second time. This time, he released the knife, and William turned Mr. Ryan over to throw punches into his face. But as he turned him, Mr. Ryan threw his knee against William, unbalancing him enough for Mr. Ryan to grab his knife again.

"You gotta do better than that, boy!"

William looked over at Anne. She looked back and her eyes met his, hers wide and shimmering with tears. The look reminded him of what was at stake. He was fighting for his future, for Liv's future, whatever the cost.

William decided he had to do the opposite of what Noah wanted to do. He wanted to stand and make Mr. Ryan come to him. Instead, he turned toward Mr. Ryan and lunged at him, trying to push the hand with the knife away with one hand as he tried to land a punch with the other. He wasn't fast enough, and blood spread like water across William's shirt, a stark red against the worn fabric. The pain was alive and unlike anything William had ever felt before. It screamed from his flesh.

William stumbled backward, his hands going to his stomach, finding the knife sunk into his flesh. He dropped to his knees, the world around him in a dizzying whirl of shadows and light. Mr. Ryan walked forward with a smile on his face, grabbing the knife handle with one hand and pushing William backward with the opposite foot. The knife withdrew with a wet sound, and cramps shot through his abdomen. William landed on his side and then rolled to his back as he fought to stay conscious. He could hear Anne crying, distant and desperate.

"Anne!" His voice was a whisper; ragged, thin, and forced from within.

Mr. Ryan stood over him, his silhouette dark against the flickering firelight Anne had managed to get lit for William's return. Mr. Ryan's weight settled over him as he straddled his waist, holding him to the floor. He gripped the knife with both hands and prepared to sink it into William's chest. Instinct took over, and both of William's hands shot up, gripping Mr. Ryan's wrists with all the strength left in him.

"Come on, son," Mr. Ryan said through clenched teeth, "this can be quick. It will only hurt for a bit."

"Anne!" William said with a grunt, locking his jaw against the pain that threatened to black him out. He could feel his muscles trembling, sweat mixing with the blood on his cheek as he held on to Mr. Ryan's arms with all he had left. The knife inched closer as William's strength faded. William's muscles burned with exhaustion, and the blade touched William's chest and drew blood as it sank in.

William let out a loud, long scream that sliced through, seeming to snap Anne out of her shock. She reached forward and pulled the gun to her. Her fingers wrapped around the cold steel of the barrel, and she turned the gun toward Mr. Ryan. Her hands trembled as she leveled the gun at Mr. Ryan's back.

"Get off him!" Anne's voice cracked, her knuckles white around the stock. Her finger hovered over the trigger, and then the shotgun roared. Mr. Ryan's body jolted forward from the impact and went limp. He fell forward, but William's arms, pushing against the trajectory of the knife, pushed Mr. Ryan to the side, away from him.

"Noah!"

William lay on the floor, his ears ringing from the gun. He coughed, and blood came with it. His life drained from him with every breath as reality slipped away.

"Hey." He groaned; a lopsided grin fought its way across his face. "Hell of a shot."

The sound of his own voice seemed distant, like the echo of someone else. He could feel consciousness leaving. It felt a lot like trying to stay awake to finish a movie after a long day. He tried to focus, but it was a losing battle. Even as his vision tunneled, the sight of Anne gave him peace.

Anne rushed to him and pressed her hands firmly on his stomach. "Noah, hold on! You're gonna be all right!"

"Anne," he said, his voice a whisper. "It's . . . it's okay." William's eyes locked onto hers. "I saved you. That's all that matters."

"Don't you dare!" Anne's scream echoed around the bare walls. She trembled, rage and fear radiating from her as she let panic take over.

Her face was streaked with tears, dirt, and blood. It was the last thing he registered. The pain let go, and he was met with total numbness. The world around him dimmed, and right when he thought everything would go black, the room spun. He looked up past Anne, and instead of the ceiling, he saw a beautiful sky full of the reds and oranges that accompanied a sunset.

CHAPTER THIRTEEN

It was like blinking. One second, he was on the floor of the old house in Green Cove; the next, he was sitting behind the wheel of a car, his car, driving. William's head was heavy with confusion, whirling as he slowly came to his senses. He reached for his stomach, and it was normal. He felt no stab wound, there was no blood, no anything. The world outside was lit up with the beautiful sunset glow during the golden hour. He blinked hard, struggling to haul his thoughts together. Liv's voice, soft yet edged with excitement, danced through the car's close interior.

"Let's pick out names for both. Just to be prepared."

He turned his head, his gaze landing on her in the passenger seat. The last rays of daylight illuminated Liv's auburn hair, making it shine. He thought about how beautiful she was and how much he'd missed her.

"William?" she said, a frown creasing her brow.

That's when it hit him. A jolt of recognition so strong it was like Mr. Ryan's knife was plunged in once again. They were on that stretch of road, the same one where everything had gone wrong the first time. His pulse raced, and then the tire exploded, echoing the one that haunted his nightmares.

"Shit!" William squeezed the wheel as he fought to keep the car from going out of control. His mind screamed in a flood of panic and urgency, trying to dredge up the memory of what he'd done before. He had to do things differently this time to save them both.

"Come on," he said to himself. The car swayed as he struggled to wrest back control. He slammed on the brakes and turned the wheel toward the side of the road. The car didn't completely agree with that plan and fishtailed.

"Will!"

The scent of burned rubber filled his nostrils as the world outside was a blur of motion. It dawned on William too late that the car had spun around, and he suddenly found that his view had shifted to face the mountain road they'd come from. His window shattered as the driver's side of the car hit the guardrail. He turned toward Liv, and he saw her looking at him with the same look he'd given her the first time.

"I love you," he managed to say, his voice barely a whisper among the groaning of crushing metal.

A series of beeps welcomed Liv to a dimly lit room in the hospital. The world was a blur, a smear of white ceiling tiles and a picture of the Colorado Front Range. No. That was a window, and it framed a surreal sight that, under normal circumstances, would have brought a smile to her face. She was in that place between sleep and awake, the place where every care in the world was gone. There was nothing but peace there. It lasted only a moment, like it always did. Her body felt like it had been dragged through hell and back, each breath an effort, every bone and muscle screaming in protest.

"Oh!" she said as the pain pulled her back to the surface of reality.

Her face felt sore and bruised, her left leg was in a temporary walking boot, and her ribs were wrapped tight, broken. She felt her stomach and began to cry.

She remembered now.

William hadn't made it. She'd miscarried.

They were together one moment, and now she was left here, alone. The doctor had said she was lucky, but she didn't see it in the same light. This felt like a life sentence to hell. A constant punch in the gut that never let up. Her hands trembled as she struggled to catch her breath.

"Can't be," she said, shaking her head, tears flooding her eyes, hot and unstoppable. "We were just talking. We were going to be . . ."

The room blurred from her tears. Liv's heart felt like an anchor sinking deep inside, dragging her down with the unbearable weight of grief. She was alone, truly alone for the first time ever. It was as if someone had ripped out her insides and left a hollow shell, echoing with the ghosts of her husband's laughter and the hope of their unborn child.

"William," she said, the name like a knife through her heart. She lay there, a tear-stained wreckage of a woman who'd had it all and lost it in a moment.

As the hours crept by, marked only by the light of the moon in the room causing the shift in shadows across the walls, Liv wrestled with the memories that came and went with each tick of the clock. William's smile, the warmth of his hand in hers, the future they'd planned. It was all gone, reduced to ashes in the blink of an eye.

"Why?" As the word escaped her lips, she felt her very soul rip. The question hung in the air, and she wasn't sure if it was a question or an accusation or maybe even a plea.

"That would be where I come in."

Liv stiffened, her heart racing. "Hello? Who's there?"

It was a man's voice, gritty from years of smoking. Looking around the room, she saw him. There, nestled in the corner, right in front of her bed, a silhouette lit by the glowing red ember of a cigar in his mouth. He puffed on the cigar and blew out a mouthful of smoke as he leaned into the moonlight. The smoke hugged his face as he smiled.

"Hello, Liv."

THE END

ABOUT THE AUTHOR

J. Nois Lane is a music industry veteran with over two decades of experience in copyright and licensing. A lifelong fan of supernatural podcasts and time travel fiction, his imagination is drawn to what lies beyond the veil of reality. *The Eternal Predicament of William J. McCoy*, inspired by a family legend, is his debut novella. Lane lives on Brindlee Mountain in North Alabama, where the fog lingers a bit longer than it should and the past is never too far away. He writes to explore the liminal spaces between the ordinary and the paranormal, and to give voice to the quiet what-ifs that haunt us all.